Praise for

Southern Spirits

This is a short, sad story of two lovers destined to be together… If you like supernatural love stories between a man and a ghost, with lots of hot sex and an education about how things work in the afterlife, you may enjoy this story. Thanks, Bailey, for giving Connor and Ro their happily ever after.
~ *Rainbow Book Reviews*

Whirlwind by Bailey Bradford was a wonderful addition to the Southern Spirits series. I always look forward to reading a book in this series and have grown to love the men in McKintock, Texas and the spirits that inhabit the town. ~ *Jeep Diva*

I really enjoyed Whirlwind and was so glad to see Stefan getting his dream and he is as wonderful as ever… I will recommend this to those who love spirits finding love, some great action, some mischief and fun, hot sexy men having steamy sex and a sweet ending ~ *MM Good Book Reviews*

Southwestern Shifters
Rescued
Relentless
Reckless
Rendered
Resilience
Reverence
Revolution
Revenge

Southern Spirits
A Subtle Breeze
When the Dead Speak
All of the Voices
Wait Until Dawn
Aftermath
What Remains

Love in Xxchange
Rory's Last Chance
Miles to Go
Bend
What Matters Most
Ex's and O's
A Bit of Me
A Bit of You
In My Arms Tonight
Where There's A Will

Leopard's Spots
Levi
Oscar
Timothy
Isaiah
Gilbert
Esau
Sullivan
Wesley
Nischal

Justice
Sabin

Mossy Glenn Ranch
Chaps and Hope
Ropes and Dreams
Saddles and Memories

Yes, Forever
Yes, Forever: Part One
Yes, Forever: Part Two
Yes, Forever: Part Three
Yes, Forever: Part Four
Yes, Forever: Part Five

Breaking the Devil

SOUTHERN SPIRITS
Volume Four

Ascension

Whirlwind

BAILEY BRADFORD

Southern Spirits Volume Four
ISBN # 978-1-78184-658-2
©Copyright Bailey Bradford 2013
Cover Art by Posh Gosh ©Copyright 2013
Interior text design by Claire Siemaszkiewicz
Totally Bound Publishing

Published in 2013 by Totally Bound Publishing, Newland House, The Point, Weaver Road, Lincoln, LN6 3QN, United Kingdom.

Totally Bound Publishing is an imprint of Total-E-Ntwined Limited.

ASCENSION

Dedication

To happily ever afters — may we all have our own.

Chapter One

"Hey, Ro, can you get the oven mitts for me?" Severo asked as he opened the oven door.

Rogelio Martinez plucked the mitts from the counter top and handed them to his uncle Sev. The heat from the oven wafted out and Ro stepped back, swiping at his brow. "Are they ready?"

"I think so." Sev pulled out the bubbling enchiladas. The spicy scent of them filled the kitchen and Ro's stomach gurgled with anticipation. Between the enchiladas and the tortillas, both homemade, he was about to drown himself in drool. He swallowed and greeted his uncle Laine as he came into the kitchen. "Hey, Uncle Laine, how was work?"

Laine took off his Stetson and held it in one hand as he walked over to Sev. The kiss they shared was brief but the love between the two men was evident in the way they leaned towards each other, and in their expressions.

Rogelio's heart pinched with something uncomfortably like jealousy. He didn't want to be ugly, and he didn't begrudge his uncles their love. He just… He wanted a love like that for himself. Well, and another man, *duh.* As he watched Sev and Laine, Ro's mind wandered to his fantasy man. Ro had pictured him so many times since he'd realised he was gay. Thick blond hair, stocky, muscular build, and a smile that promised all kinds of mischief.

Ro blinked and shook his head. The image forming in his mind wasn't one of a man he'd ever had. It was of a picture he'd seen years ago when, as a teen, he'd gone snooping into Sev's past. It had twined with Laine's, and Ro had been a naïve and romantic young fool, so entranced by Sev and Laine's love story that he hadn't been able to think of much else.

"You gonna help set the table, kid?"

Laine's deep rumbling voice snapped Ro out of his thoughts. "Yeah, sure."

Ro took the plain blue plates down from the shelf and placed them on the table. It didn't take him long to lay out silverware and glasses of sweet tea. Laine made up a batch of guacamole while Sev finished up the salsa. They sat down at the table once everything was in place.

Laine arched a brow at him and pointed at the enchiladas. "Two or three?"

"Three." Ro was thin as a whip but he could and did eat anything he wanted.

Sev sniffed at him. "I used to have that kind of metabolism. It'll catch up to you, trust me."

"I doubt that," Ro said as he scooped some guacamole onto his plate. He was starving, but he could spare a moment to pick on his uncle. "You're still in shape, and you're getting old."

Sev hissed and kicked him under the table. "I am *not* old, smart ass. And Laine's older than me, anyway!"

Ro nodded and managed not to grimace as his shin took another kick. "Yeah, but Laine has always looked..." Ro waited for Laine to glare at him, then he sent Laine his sweetest smile. "Dignified."

Laine snorted and muttered, "Dignified, my ass. Sayin' I always looked old is what you're sayin'."

Ro hitched up a shoulder and shovelled a forkful of enchiladas into his mouth. He closed his eyes and moaned appreciatively as the hot cheese almost burnt his tongue. He wasn't the only one enjoying the meal, either. The three men quit picking on each other and settled in to eat.

A prickling sensation caused the hairs on the back of Ro's neck to stand up. His skin flushed with an awareness that he'd come to recognise. Sev cocked his head, but Laine kept eating, right up until the time that his plate scooted away from him.

Laine grabbed his plate and glared around the room. "Aw, damn it, Conner! You're just jealous because you can't have any!"

Sev shook his head. "He can have yours," he said just as Laine's plate was lifted off the table.

Laine leapt up from his seat but the plate spun up until its contents almost touched the ceiling.

"Conner..." Laine growled.

Ro's pulse raced and he grew warm in places he just shouldn't while sitting at his uncles' table. Ro set his fork down and pressed his hands to his thighs, digging his fingertips hard against his legs to distract himself from the wave of arousal washing over him. Only someone like him would have a crush on a dead guy with a love for pranks.

"I'm gonna call someone who can exorcise spirits," Laine warned. The plate tipped precariously and

Laine tossed a hand out. "I was kidding! You know we love you, buddy."

And just like that, the plate was lowered to the table again. Ro watched enviously as Laine's hair was tousled. Sev swatted at the air shortly thereafter. "Conner, don't fuck with my hair—urgh!" Sev's hair became the victim of a mini whirlwind. Laine snickered. Ro dipped his head and wished he'd been included in the playing, but, as usual, Conner didn't seem to notice him. He supposed that shouldn't be surprising. Conner had been Laine's lover before dying. There was no reason for the prankster spirit to notice Ro's existence.

What would be the point if he did? Ro couldn't figure that one out. He kept his sigh to himself. He was just a geeky twenty-eight-year-old who still lived at home with his parents and didn't have a life to speak of.

"Did you sense him?" Sev asked as Ro fiddled with a fold in his jeans.

Ro shook his head. "No." He didn't think that prickling sensation counted. As much as he'd longed to be gifted like Sev, to be able to communicate with the dead, Ro just wasn't able to. He figured his familiarity with Conner was the only reason he knew when that particular spirit popped in. Conner had been swooping in to tease Laine and Sev, and sometimes save their asses in certain situations, for a long time now. Ro had heard so many stories—

Sev pushed back his chair. "I bet he's in the bathroom hiding my stuff again. I'll be right back."

"Huh?" Ro looked at Laine for an explanation.

Laine grunted around a mouthful of food. He chewed it then swallowed, in no obvious hurry to answer, but he finally did. "'Huh' isn't exactly a question, at least not in my mind, it isn't. Conner's taken to hiding Sev's creams and hair dye. I don't think he likes your uncle hiding his grey." Laine took a drink of his tea and held the condensation-covered glass in his hand as he spoke. His dark eyes held a seriousness to them that made Ro want to squirm like a recalcitrant child. "You're a smart kid. Are you gonna keep working at Virginia's Café forever?"

In other words, why didn't he go to college, get a real job—no, a career—and make something of his life? Ro felt a surge of anger at that. He'd been asked it too often. He tipped his chin up and glared at Laine, fighting down a shiver of fear and the intimidation he always felt at even the idea of standing up to the sheriff. But Ro was tired of everyone looking at him like he was a fool for not wanting more.

"What's wrong with it if I do? I'm making an honest living. I'm good with the customers." It wasn't challenging, except for when Mr Brown decided to be an asshole, but even that Ro could handle. "Not everyone is made to go to college. There have to be little people working jobs like mine so educated people can have food they don't have to cook themselves. It's not like—"

"Whoa, whoa, kid, stop," Laine said as he held up a hand. "I didn't mean any offence."

Ro cocked his head, puzzled by that. "Well, how else was I supposed to take it?"

"Maybe that your uncle Laine thinks you're too smart and talented to spend the rest of your life waiting on tables?" Sev said from behind him.

Ro twisted around in his chair to watch Sev stash an armful of products in the pantry. "Won't Conner find them there?"

"Nah. He's off again, probably keeping Stefan company, or spying on someone else." Sev closed the pantry door and leaned a hip against it. "You're evading."

Ro scowled and turned back to his plate. "No, I'm not. I already answered. I don't want to go anywhere other than where I am. Why's that so hard for anyone to understand? Some people go and come back, some people just go, and some people stay and are happy with their lives." Honestly, Ro wasn't a hundred per cent certain why he didn't want to go off to college, or even to the community college. It just wasn't for him. That was the best he could come up with.

Sev sat down beside him and touched his nape, brushing aside Ro's long hair to do so. "Look, we just worry. We only want you happy, just like your mama and dad do. They love you, but feel like you're staying here because you feel obligated."

"I don't." He did, but that wasn't all of it. His mother's diabetes had ravaged her body over the past decade. The amputations and dialysis were draining what had remained of her will to live, Ro could see it. So could his father Roger and Ro's siblings.

And so could Sev. Ro saw the sadness Sev tried to hide. It had etched lines around his eyes and mouth, and dimmed the enthusiasm that used to shine so bright in Sev's eyes.

"Someone has to be here for them," Ro finally said when he couldn't stand another moment of silence. "One of their kids should, at least, and I won't ask that of my sister or brother. They have dreams that don't involve staying in McKinton, and I really do like my job."

"But—" Sev began and Ro was done arguing.

"No, Sev. I don't have the drive, the...the ambition that I'd need to do something else. I'm comfortable here. It's where I want to be, even if that means living with my parents. They need me, no matter what they say." Truly, the only thing he'd wanted was to be like Sev, but he wasn't, not really. Sev could have been his father, they were so alike in looks, both on the short side with slender builds and dark glossy black hair. Well, Ro's was natural, while he suspected, now, that Sev's had some help courtesy of L'Oréal. Sev was also more muscular, but they had the same green-grey eyes and honey-coloured skin. Celadon, that was the name of the colour, if he wanted to get technical about it. Sharing those traits with Sev had given Ro so much hope that he'd inherit more things from Sev, but he hadn't, and that was that.

"Let's just enjoy our meal and stop harping on him," Laine rumbled. "Sorry, Ro, since I'm the one that started it."

Ro rolled his neck once Sev moved his hand. He got a good pop out of it and grinned when that sound made Laine wince. "It's not the first time I've heard it. I'm over it." He cast a teasing glance at Sev. "So, how long have you been dying that grey?"

Ro grinned as Sev shook his fork at Laine. "You told!"

Satisfied with the distraction he'd created, Ro sat back and enjoyed the show.

Chapter Two

The thing about being dead was that he really lost track of time. Understandable, Conner supposed, considering time didn't affect him anymore.

Well, not him personally, as in his spirit form. But it did affect him in other ways, like when he had to watch those he'd left behind in life. To see them age, and grow frail—

Laine would shit bricks if he knew what Conner was thinking. Laine wouldn't know, though. Conner could communicate with his former lover to an extent, but, for the most part, the art of conversation was lost between the veil of the living and the dead.

Severo, Laine's partner—and Conner couldn't have picked a better-suited man for Laine had he tried...which, okay, he might have meddled some— could communicate with spirits somewhat. The bond with Conner was the strongest, and that was owing in part to Conner's determination to have a relationship with Laine. To do so entailed having one with Sev, and maybe Conner had been a little—or a lot—jealous at first, but Sev had come to mean a lot to Conner over the years. Plus, Sev loved Laine, *really* loved him like Conner wished he had before he'd died.

Still, Conner had loved Laine enough to die for him, although if he'd been given a choice, he'd have lived and kept Laine safe, too. Whether or not they'd have made it together for the rest of their lives, Conner couldn't say. Sometimes he thought not, because they'd been so closeted, but who was to say how Fate would have played out if Conner hadn't been murdered by a stalker who'd wanted to possess Laine?

It didn't help to wonder. Conner had long since stopped doing so because watching Laine and Sev had finally stopped making him hurt with that sharp edge of want, and had started comforting him. It was good to see them happy and loving each other. Hot, too, although Conner tried not to spy on them when they were having sex…now. He had been a bit of a Peeping Tom for a while, but he knew Laine and Sev hadn't minded. In fact, he thought once they'd got past the idea of him being Laine's ex, him watching had added a bit of spice now and then.

Now, it was hard for Conner to watch them. He'd started noticing things like the almost solid grey of Laine's hair and the wrinkles lining Sev's face, although the man battled them with every cream he could find. They weren't so deep or numerous, but they were there, along with strands of grey that Sev dyed black every month so they would match the rest of his hair.

At first Conner had been amused, and had taken great pleasure in teasing Sev, hiding his dye and spreading his face cream on the mirror to look like…well, lots of things. Conner could easily get restless, distracted, and once he'd got the hang of making parts of himself substantial enough to move things in the living world, he'd kind of gone overboard.

He was just astounded because it seemed like yesterday that he'd been thinking about how he used to watch Laine and Sev and admire their firm bodies and their sheer livingness. How many years had he been dead now? Conner looked at the table where Laine had left the newspaper spread out.

Good old Laine, he'll never upgrade to reading the news online. He used to get print smudges on his cheek and chin when – Conner stopped the thought more out of habit than anything else. Once it would have made him ache with regret and lost love, but those sensations had long ago ceased occurring, maybe because he had stopped letting himself think on what he'd lost when he'd been murdered.

That whole nasty episode wasn't something he'd ever forget. He wondered if he'd have felt any better about dying if he'd known spirits existed back then. Conner had known he wouldn't live to escape his situation before he actually died. It had been so obvious in the glee his killer took in torturing him. Sometimes he could still feel that knife piercing his skin and muscle so, so slowly, trailing agony behind it and racing terror in front of it. Conner had lived for hours under that sadistic bastard's blade. He had literally got off on torturing Conner to death.

That last probably explained why, though he'd enjoyed watching Laine and Sev and some other people having sex, it hadn't really occurred to him that he could do any such thing. After all, if, when you died, you were free from physical pain – except in your memory – and able to zip around the world, *and* get to fuck? Where was the downside to dying then?

Granted, not everyone who died turned into a lingering spirit, but some did.

What would happen if two lovers, completely devoted to each other, died, and only one was a spirit? Conner shivered, more of a wispy movement for him but the same concept, he thought. He didn't know where the people went who didn't hang around post-death. And he didn't want to find out. Conner liked being where he was. Going somewhere…else scared him.

Maybe that was why he was still on the planet.

Conner's musings ceased when Sev and his nephew came in through the front door. Conner had had what he called 'jumpy brain' lately, his mind not being able to focus on any one thing for long.

For the first several years after his death, Conner had been unable to concentrate for long. He just wanted to have fun, but he'd been able to focus when it'd been important to do so. Death had made him more of a flighty person than he'd been in life. Once he'd realised that, it had started to bug him. He didn't want to be vapid in form and personality both.

So he'd started trying to have more substance, started paying attention to those around him more. Part of it was that he'd taken an innocent spirit under his wing, so to speak, and the rest was that he couldn't deny the changes in those living people he cared about.

Just like his worries and observations about Laine and Sev aging, and yes, whether or not those two would get to be together in death, either in spirit form or wherever they'd go after. Conner worried, but he just couldn't focus on it. To do so made him jittery. He'd even dropped Sev's ridiculously expensive eye cream a few days ago when he'd just meant to hide it behind the towels. Jesus, Sev could shriek.

He could also laugh and sound just as young as he'd been all those years ago when Conner had been a lost and terrified spirit with a message he'd needed to get to Laine about who had killed him. Hearing that laugh made Conner warm inside, so he floated up to the ceiling, his spiritual form no more substantial than the air that he let hold him up. Less, actually, he guessed. He'd always sucked at physics. All he could say for sure was he was up.

And that it wasn't just Sev's laugh that made Conner want to hang around and observe for a while. Though it made him feel like a skeevy pervert, he couldn't force himself to disappear when Sev's nephew, Rogelio Martinez, was around. The boy was beautiful, and Conner knew he wasn't really a boy, having had an eighteenth birthday party some time ago. Years, but how many, he couldn't remember. Enough that Rogelio's form, though lithe and on the short side — yeah, even in death, Conner wouldn't have admitted that to the kid — was obviously that of an adult. It showed in the slight delineation of muscle and the confidence with which Rogelio carried himself.

When Conner was around him lately, all the memories of arousal that he had suppressed tried to come back to the surface. He'd learnt that touching another spirit felt like he remembered it did when touching as living beings. He just hadn't applied that to a sexual manner of touching. Possibly because his main companion in the spirit world was Stefan, who, despite having died as an adult at nineteen, still seemed like a kid to Conner.

Part of that was because Stefan had been… Conner searched for the politically correct term. Things had changed a lot since he'd died, and he liked trying to keep current. *Intellectually challenged?* Conner shrugged. Stefan didn't seem so different now, as if death had freed him of the physical limitations of his body and mind. He'd always be a kid to Conner, though.

"And so will Rogelio," Conner murmured, needing to hear himself say it. Sev cocked his head and frowned and Conner slapped a hand to his own forehead. He knew Sev could hear him on some level. Sometimes he heard him clearly. Other times, like today, hopefully, not so much.

Sev held a hand up to shush Rogelio, who glanced nervously around the room and whispered, "Is *he* here?"

That wasn't a thrill he felt at hearing Rogelio enquire about him. The kid wasn't interested in him. For God's sake, he was *dead!* That was probably it. Morbid fascination on Rogelio's part. Conner wasn't around the kid constantly, because even dead, he had a life. So to speak. He'd deliberately kept himself from teasing Rogelio, because—well, he wasn't sure why. Probably because it was Sev and Laine who were Conner's friends, and Rogelio had been an awkward teenage boy when he'd moved to McKinton. God, Conner wasn't sure of anything right then as Rogelio turned his head towards him.

Rogelio's eyes widened when he looked to where Conner was floating. Conner twitched, feeling that gaze like a heated breeze over his skin. It was too weird, too…intense for him. Conner zipped himself right out of the house, popping in instead on Laine in his office.

Laine, still handsome, still sheriff, but damn, he was sure looking his age. Conner tried to figure out how old that was exactly but gave up when he spotted Laine twirling his tin star badge on the desk top. That was Conner's job!

It didn't take much more than a thought to have the star shooting out of Laine's hand and doing slow, steady circles in front of Laine's scowling face.

"Conner, I'm trying to think here." Laine smiled when he said it, though, and leant back in his chair as he watched the star. "That's a neat trick. I've never gotten tired of it after all these years. You should do that at my retirement party. Scare the shit out of the incoming sheriff."

Great, I've established myself as a cheesy entertainment source in my afterlife. Conner swatted the star into the trash can, put out at being seen as nothing more than a party trick.

"Aw, stop pouting. You weren't this moody before," Laine drawled. He leaned over the arm of his chair and plucked the star out of the trash bin. "You know you mean more to me than a lot of living people."

Before. Conner hated that word. 'Before' meant when he had been a living, breathing man. When he had been bound by gravity and morals and his own physical restraints. 'Before' meant what he'd lost, and he couldn't dwell on that. It caused a confusing mix of emotions that he didn't want to trudge through. He did stop pouting. There wasn't any point to it. Laine was Laine, and he'd never been deliberately mean or particularly gifted with words.

"I think Matt'll make a good sheriff, don't you?"

Conner sat on the edge of Laine's desk. He reached over and tapped Laine's hand, a bare touch that Laine probably only felt as a tingling sensation. It was enough, though. Laine smiled crookedly and pinned the star back onto his shirt. "Sev's been wanting to go places, you know. Well, I'm sure you do know, much as you and him do your chatting thing. He's nervous about leaving his sister and them behind, but I think they'll be all right."

'Them' being not only Alma but Roger and Rogelio as well. Conner supposed he could pop in on them more often. There wasn't much he could do besides that. It wasn't like any of Sev's family had his talent for communicating with the dead.

Conner remembered the way Rogelio had just been looking at him—well, maybe not at him, but still—just a few minutes ago. That had to be pure luck. Rogelio hadn't ever seemed to be sensitive to his presence before then, not unless Sev or Laine mentioned Conner being there. Or unless Conner decided to goose his friends or some other such prank in front of Sev's family.

At least Sev's sister Alma had finally quit crossing herself every time anyone mentioned Conner's name. Jesus, he wasn't evil incarnate, just a dead guy who got bored too often. Conner shivered thinking of Alma and her body mutilated by necessity as the disease ravaged her. It wouldn't be long before she joined him, and he couldn't decide whether it'd be a good thing or not for Sev to be there when that happened.

Conner listened to Laine ramble on until another deputy, Rich, came into Laine's office. Conner wasn't up to messing with Rich. That guy had had it bad enough, almost dying at the hand of the same psycho who'd killed Conner.

It was weird, how he had more of a family in death than he'd had while alive, Conner mused as he searched for Stefan. Usually he found the younger spirit hanging around Stefan's brother Lee, and his partner Darren. Conner could add all of them to his friends list, too. When he'd been alive, he'd been outgoing and popular, but he hadn't had many close friends. Well, one, really, and that'd been Laine. He'd been so deep in the closet, he hadn't been able to risk letting anyone besides his lover too close.

Granted, he couldn't communicate with most of the people he popped in on, but they almost all knew about him. When he let them know he was there—if he let them know, generally by tumbling things in the air that shouldn't be tumbling in the air—they greeted him with a warmth he didn't think any of his friends from his living time had. Except for Laine, when they had been alone.

Today was just going to be one of those days, he supposed. The past kept bubbling up in his mind, and a sense of melancholy and loneliness pervaded his normally happy persona no matter how much he tried not to let it.

Stefan was laughing, his eyes lit up with joy as he zipped along beside Lee. Conner didn't want to intrude, not when he was feeling every bit the moody mess Laine had called him out on being. He settled his feet on the ground, pretending for just one moment that he was alive again, that he didn't have to concentrate to feel the hardness of the earth beneath his feet. He glanced up at the brilliant blue sky, squinted at the sun's glare that, even though he was a spirit, still made his eyes burn and water. He would never figure out stuff like that. He only knew it happened, that his spiritual body could still feel and his heart could ache with loneliness.

Conner looked down at the ground. He saw his boots, his favourite pair he'd worn so often when he'd been alive. Faded denim jeans hugged his legs, and a tight blue T-shirt covered his upper body. Why was he even wearing clothes? He was dead, and they weren't real. Stefan was clothed, too, and all the other spirits he'd seen were as well. Had he manufactured the clothes when he'd been in that place between death and dying?

This is getting too deep for me. Conner had been moderately intelligent at best. There was no way he was going to figure out all this afterlife shit. It was a sign of how bored he was that he was even trying. Conner snorted at himself, at his stupid fancies, trying to pretend he was human and whole again. His eyes burned more from the damned sun, that was all it was, and he shot up into the air like a just-fired missile. He wasn't trying to flee from his thoughts — that never worked — but if he could just lose himself in the beauty around him for a while, he'd take it. It was the only thing he could really have anymore.

Chapter Three

Ro couldn't explain it, but he had felt the oddest sensation when he'd been talking to Sev. It was almost like he'd heard a buzzing in his head, then Sev had shushed him and Ro had known Conner was in the room. It was kind of like the way he'd felt the other day at dinner when Conner had shown up, but this time it was more intense.

Conner Sutherland. Ro had of course heard stories about Laine's deceased lover. He'd even Googled the man years ago. The horrific account of Conner's death had made him cry. The tragic parting of lovers had twisted his youthful heart into a knot of regret for Laine and Conner.

Then Ro had met Laine, and seen how much Sev loved him, and vice versa. He supposed it was fate or something that had brought Laine and Sev together. Or Conner. Ro liked to think Conner had loved Laine enough to want him to be happy in this life.

Ro pulled a file out of his desk drawer. He'd put the clippings together what seemed like ages ago, when he'd been a young, dumb kid full of romantic idealism. He snorted at that innocent boy now. The only romance he'd ever have would be in his head unless he left the town of McKinton. Gay men weren't exactly falling off tree limbs here. Ro snickered, imagining sexy studs floating to the ground like leaves on a fall breeze. McKinton would become a very popular town if that were to happen.

Inside the folder were articles Ro had printed out and clippings from actual newspapers. Different cases were tagged with coloured tabs, but it was the blue ones he found himself fingering. Ro didn't know whether to be amused by himself or disgusted. Maybe he was pathetic for not wanting to leave town and have a different life, but he didn't care. He had to do what his conscience told him to. And he had to listen to his heart. He'd tried ignoring both a time or two, and, granted, that'd been out of sexual curiosity, but what a disaster each one had been.

Ro pulled out the picture he'd been seeking. The colours were fading on it, but he could still see Conner's blond hair and bright blue eyes well enough. There was that secretive smile, and it just hurt Ro to know the man's life had been cut short. *Here's a man who had more to offer the world…*

A knock on his bedroom door startled Ro into slamming the folder shut without tucking Conner's picture away. "Yeah?" he called out as he set the papers down and leapt up from his chair.

"Son, can I come in?"

"Sure, Dad. It's not locked." Ro opened the door, though, because his dad wouldn't ever just walk in. Once Ro had turned eighteen, he'd been afforded as much privacy as he could have when still living in his parents' home.

His dad looked old, and tired. Ro's breath hitched as he asked, "How'd Mom's appointment go today?" Normally he'd have checked in on her himself, but her door had been shut and his dad had been in there with her.

Roger walked in and sat on Ro's bed, slumping as if his shoulders couldn't carry their burdens any longer. Roger was only twenty-one years older than Ro, but he looked like a man in his sixties rather than in his late forties just then.

Roger ran a hand down his face, then curled his fingers into a fist and rubbed at one eye. "Dr Hebert doesn't think she'll be—" Roger's voice broke, his breath catching on a sob. Ro darted to the bed and sat beside his father, embracing him awkwardly owing to their positioning. "He doesn't think she'll make it more than a few months. Her kidneys are barely functioning, and Alma wouldn't accept a transplant even if she were eligible."

"No, she always said she wouldn't," Ro murmured. His mama was terrified that her loved ones would develop the same disease she had, and wasn't willing to let them donate a kidney when it might very well cost them their life later on. Add to the diabetes the heart disease that was killing her and there was no hope left for Ro. He couldn't stop the tears, and didn't care that he was almost thirty, sobbing in his father's arms. They were going to lose his mama, and he'd never be ashamed of mourning that, of mourning her.

Roger cried right along with him, great sobs that shook the bed even if they weren't very loud. Neither of them would risk Alma hearing them. Ro felt scalded inside, as if he'd been made raw from the pain of knowing the loss they'd soon face. It wasn't a surprise—they'd had years to see it coming, but there simply was no way to truly prepare for the loss of someone you loved so much.

"I need to call your brother and sister," Roger said some time later, the words tickling over the top of Ro's head as his dad's exhale ruffled his hair.

"I can —" Ro started but his dad cut him off.

"No, it's my job as their papa," Roger said. He tugged gently on Ro's long hair until Ro looked up at him. Roger's eyes were swollen and red, as was his nose, but he was still the big, strong man Ro had always admired. "You can go sit with your mama for a while, if you want to. She's sleeping, but…"

But it might be one of the last chances Ro had to be alone with her. He couldn't force himself to ask anything more specific, the child in him still wanting his parents. It didn't matter how old you were, he couldn't imagine it was easy to lose the people who'd loved you unquestioningly and supported your hopes and dreams. Ro sniffed and got up. He went into his bathroom as his dad left with a quiet murmur.

Ro checked his reflection in the mirror and grimaced. He looked like shit, with an almost bruised tint to the skin under his eyes. His face was ruddy and his nose red. He looked away and turned on the faucet. After splashing his face, he got that weird sensation again, as if he were being watched. Ro tipped his head to one side and contemplated the feeling. It was like an electrical current sparking up and down his spine, sending streams of awareness throughout his body.

Was it Conner? Ro wiped his face on the towel then blew his nose, cheeks going hot as he did so. How embarrassing would it be to have Conner see him cleaning out his sinuses?

"Don't be an idiot," Ro muttered to himself. He wasn't being watched, he was just a mess after that talk with his dad. Ro's eyes burned, tears threatening again. He grabbed the towel and pressed it to his eyes, fighting to stem the tears that didn't seem to want to be dammed. "Stop it, stop it, stop it," he chanted, until finally the words seemed to penetrate and he was able to blink back the excess moisture.

Ro realised something then. That electric sensation was still thrumming through him, and… He gasped as he dropped the towel. Something that felt very much like a hand was stroking his hair.

As soon as he gasped it stopped. "Conner?" he whispered, his skin pebbling with goose bumps all over. Ro still felt it, not the touch but that thrumming. He felt like all kinds of a fool, looking all over the bathroom. He knew he wasn't going to *see* Conner, but Conner could see him, and Ro couldn't think of any other spirit that would be popping up.

Then he realised he was just being a fool indeed. Conner had never come around him before. It was stupid of him to think the man would do so now. And dead or not, Conner was a man to Ro. He would always be that handsome, charismatic-looking guy from the newspaper clipping that Ro had ogled for over a decade now.

Ro laughed out loud at that. How ridiculous was it that he'd spent almost half of his life crushing on a dead guy? No wonder he'd never had more than a couple of unsatisfactory quickies. He'd let his teenage romanticism rule his adult life, and he was only now realising it. Maybe if he hadn't been so content to just plod along—but he had been, and he was. There was nowhere else for him to be but where he lived right then. Ro had no desire to move away from McKinton, or from his family.

But he didn't have to be pathetic and start hallucinating about someone who'd been dead for ages and who had never bothered to appear to him in any manner before. Best to stop that before he ended up in a psychiatric hospital. Ro shuddered, remembering Sev talking about being put in just such an institution as a child. Sev's parents hadn't believed that he could speak to the dead, had thought he was just insane.

Or else they'd just wanted him silenced. Ro thought that was more likely. He remembered his grandparents, and they weren't nice people at all. Ro hadn't seen them since he'd moved to McKinton a dozen years ago.

That odd sensation was gone, he realised. Ro was mildly disappointed, but put that down to his mental state. He was going to lose his mother soon, and he was lonely even surrounded by family.

Ro left the bathroom, not really thinking about anything at that point. He stopped, stunned and suddenly mortified. The file folder he'd set aside was open, its contents spread neatly on the bed. Conner's picture was there on top, surrounded by all the snippets and printouts of everything else having to do with his case. Before Ro could figure out what that meant, chaos erupted in his room. A maelstrom of paper spun in rapid circles above his bed. The sounds of it whistling through the air were punctuated with ripping noises as bits of paper were shredded.

"Stop!" Ro shrieked before he thought to censor himself. He ran and started grabbing at the papers. "Stop it! Damn it, *stop!* This is all I have—" Ro bit his tongue, hard enough to taste blood, but better that than finishing what he'd been about to say if Conner was the one creating the mess in Ro's room. He would have died of embarrassment if he'd blurted out that the flying papers were all he had of a man he'd never have, of a man he measured all other potential lovers by. Stupid, he knew, but it was what it was. Ro couldn't seem to prevent the infatuation he'd harboured for so long.

"Please," he said as the papers kept being ripped to shreds. He caught one and saw that it was a piece of the news article about Conner's brutal death. Ro was truly mortified and sorry. He could understand Conner being upset at seeing it. "Conner...please stop. I'm sorry, okay? I didn't mean to upset you."

The papers spun around again, but within seconds the speed had dropped until they were barely moving in the air. Then they dropped, all but one. Ro watched as the picture of Conner rotated to a stop several feet above the bed. He didn't feel that electric current so much as it seemed to be a part of him just then, just as his blood and lungs and heart were. The picture crinkled slightly, the paper bowing as if someone were stroking over it. Was Conner looking, remembering? Did one remember who and what they were when they died, if they stayed on Earth?

So many questions, and Ro couldn't ask them. Even if he could, Conner couldn't answer. He thought it had to be Conner there with him, though the why of Conner's appearance eluded him.

The picture shook, then it was snapped hard, the edges of it going taut just before it dropped to the bed. There was an almost palpable withdrawal of the force that'd been there, like a vacuum sucking power out of the room, and Ro knew he was alone again. Alone, and rattled, and in dire need of a hand-vac, because

Conner had shredded every damn piece of paper except the one with his picture on it. Ro was grateful for that, at least.

C h a p t e r   F o u r

So much for thinking he didn't get bent out of shape over his past. Conner huddled in the corner of Ro's room, shrinking down into the smallest, darkest patch of shadows he could find. He'd thought—well, it didn't matter what he'd thought.

Conner had been bored, and remembered that he should try to check in on Alma and Roger more often, and Ro, of course. Alma had looked perilously close to crossing over to his side of existence, or on to Heaven or Hell or wherever. It'd been too depressing, so Conner had popped in on Ro and found the young man a mess.

A very sexy mess, and Conner had wanted to comfort him. He ached in a way he couldn't remember feeling, though it reminded him of Laine for some weird reason. Before he knew it, he had been stroking Ro's hair. Conner had had to concentrate, but he'd managed to feel the silky strands, the warmth of a living body close to his ethereal one. Faint beginnings of arousal had begun shortly thereafter, causing Conner's dick to fill. That had been surprising, although he'd been turned on sometimes when he'd peeked on Laine and Sev. Just, it hadn't ever been enough to make him truly horny. Sex hadn't been a pressing need in years, obviously, but Conner had found himself suddenly wanting to bury his hard cock in Ro's ass.

Which, in turn, had made him feel like a total perv. Conner hadn't been able to leave even then. Maybe, if he'd just been wanting to fuck Ro, he could have, but there were memories of Ro over the past years that had embedded themselves in Conner's heart. He'd kept away from Ro for so long, especially after that one time he'd peeked and found Ro in the alley behind Virginia's Café with that...that scumbag. Conner had wanted to kill the man fucking Ro's sweet mouth. It had infuriated him, and had scared him because of the intensity of his reaction.

Conner had told himself it was because he'd watched Ro grow up, but there, in Ro's bathroom, Conner had kind of faced the truth. It was depressing and awful, but he thought he might be a little bit in love with Ro. Maybe it was just years of familiarity, or maybe it was simply loneliness. Conner knew Ro was lonely. How could he not be? And Conner himself was finding out that he wanted more than just to haunt and tease his living friends. He was glad to help them, and happy to have saved their lives a few times—but he was dead, and they weren't. They all had someone, and he had...Stefan, who was a good friend, along with some other spirits. Was that all he'd ever get to have?

He'd freaked upon seeing the file Ro had on him. The clippings were old, Conner had seen the dates on some of them. Something inside him had snapped. He didn't want Ro pitying him, and didn't want Ro thinking of him as the poor, dumb idiot who'd got himself tied up and carved into pieces.

Seeing the picture of himself had been like being tossed from a hot skillet into a bucket of ice. Conner had had such a mix of emotions in him then as he'd looked at that picture, and now as he thought about it. He tried really hard not to think about what-ifs or dwell on regrets for past mistakes. All that did was depress him.

But seeing himself in that picture—he'd kind of forgotten what he'd looked like. It was odd, really. Now that he thought about it, he hadn't seen his own reflection since he'd come into his current state of existence. He was sure he had an appearance, because he saw Stefan and other spirits. They looked like people to him, like living people except the colours of them were muted somewhat. And, of course, they could go all in spirit form, floating and disappearing, turning into balls of light or ripples of colour on the breeze.

Had he just not cared to see himself? Could he see himself? That was easier to deal with than thinking about Ro and the confusing feelings that had arisen then. Conner zipped over to Sev and Laine's. He immediately felt like a self-centred asshole when he saw Laine holding Sev on the couch as Sev cried quietly.

Shit. He must have got an update on Alma. Conner didn't hesitate, making his way to his friends and sending out comforting thoughts as he concentrated on touching them both. Death was a hard thing to deal with, and he wished he could do something for them.

"If…" Sev sniffled and rubbed his nose on Laine's chest before continuing. "Conner, if she joins you, tell me, okay? Can... Can you make her stay, like you did?"

Conner found the words he wanted—they always seemed to be floating in the air when he tried to speak to someone who was alive—and pushed the words at Sev. *"No. I don't even know how I ended up here. If I could, I would do anything to help you."*

It was strangely like growing up, a rapid maturation that had Conner feeling all of his years then, the living ones along with his spirit years as well. Seeing so much pain in his friend's expression, in Laine's, too, changed something inside him.

Pranks didn't seem nearly so interesting after that, and for a solid week he didn't bother teasing anyone. Instead he sat back and observed the mourning process when Alma passed quicker than anyone had expected. She didn't linger, her soul bright and vibrant as it shot up farther than Conner could see, and he was too afraid to chase after it. He didn't want to go wherever it was she went. The idea scared him to his core. Sev cried harder when Conner told him Alma wasn't with him.

"At least she isn't suffering anymore," people told Alma's loved ones at various times. Conner knew that was small comfort if it was any comfort at all. Sev seemed to have aged almost overnight, and Conner realised his friend had stopped bothering to colour over the grey streaks in his hair.

Conner tried to shake Sev out of his funk, planting hair dye bottles in various places, but after Sev poured a bottle of it down the drain and stomped off, Conner gave up. He couldn't help Sev, it seemed.

Nor could he ease Ro's pain. Conner kept his distance, because he wanted so badly not to. He wanted to swoop in and hold Ro, to comfort him like

Laine comforted Sev more and more now. But Ro seemed untouchable in his grief.

Conner had had to stop checking on Ro the third time he'd found him in the alley with a stranger. Conner hadn't hung around long enough to see who it was, had just noted a dark shape grunting as he slammed into Ro's ass over and over. Conner had felt sick and angry. He'd fled before he could do something he'd probably not regret, like using the trash can to beat the guy who was fucking Ro. With his luck, he'd accidentally have killed the asshole and ended up spending eternity fighting him in the afterlife.

After that, Conner forced himself to stay away from Ro like he had for years. He tried to, at least, but sometimes he slipped and would find himself watching Ro through the windows of Virginia's Café, or visiting with Sev and Laine. Conner didn't know how much time passed, but Sev seemed to recover somewhat from the loss of his sister. The grey streaks were once again dyed over, and eventually he began to laugh, that spark lighting his pretty eyes like it had before.

But Ro… He only seemed to grieve more. Conner couldn't help but notice that Ro looked worn and thin, as if he weren't sleeping at night or eating enough. It broke his heart, which alternately surprised him and shocked him. He hadn't thought he'd truly felt so strongly for Ro. Maybe he had even thought he was too flighty to feel such strong emotions for someone besides Laine and Sev.

He thought about how it had hurt, losing Laine, not only when he'd died, but to another man. Granted, Conner had kind of pushed Sev and Laine together, but that was only after he'd concluded that he wanted

Laine to be happy, and that Sev was the man to make him so. Didn't mean it hadn't hurt the first time the two had struck sparks off each other. Conner had been jealous, and careless, and he'd almost killed Sev in his confusion.

Conner didn't want to feel like that again. If he stayed away from Ro completely, maybe he'd get over the guy. To that end, Conner tried to find someone else who turned him on. In the spirit world, there was no one. Stefan was cute enough, but Conner couldn't shake the image of him as a little brother. The other spirits in the nearby vicinity were either straight or female, neither of which would work for him, obviously. It occurred to him that he didn't have to stay right there in McKinton. While he seriously doubted there was a spirit-world version of a gay club where he could go and get laid, there had to be some way of hooking up with others like himself.

It was the idea of the gay club that guided him. Conner was considering it as he leaned against a tree on the outskirts of McKinton. Stefan found him there, lighting down beside him and grinning happily.

"What are you thinking about, Conner? You look so serious, and that's just weird."

Conner growled at Stefan right before he tickled the younger man. Stefan squealed and batted at his hands, but Conner dug his fingertips in against Stefan's ribs.

"Stop! Oh my God, I'm gonna pee!" Stefan laughed and Conner stopped tickling him long enough to cock an eyebrow at Stefan.

"You do know we don't pee?"

Stefan huffed and tossed his head back as if he had a mane of flowing hair rather than the short spiky poufs he'd always had. "Duh, unless you want to pee, then you can."

"What are you talking about?" Conner asked, feeling stupid. He'd been a spirit longer than Stefan, so he should have known more, which meant Stefan was pulling his leg.

"I'm not screwing with you. Just 'cuz we're dead doesn't mean we can't do things like pee or beat off." Stefan rubbed his palm over his crotch as if to emphasise those points. "It doesn't mean our dicks don't work."

"You're just messing with me," Conner told him, but he had a bad feeling he'd just been willingly ignorant. He'd been able to get hard, once he'd bothered to give enough of a damn to do so. He was considering going and trying to find someone.

"Am not." Stefan unzipped his pants and pulled out his cock.

"Stefan!" Conner wasn't a prude but that was just…wrong.

"Stop being such an old fart." Stefan aimed his shaft. "Now, I don't really feel like I need to do this, but I guess I just always enjoyed taking a piss before, so it didn't occur to me I couldn't do it here." Conner didn't want to look, but he had to. Sure enough a stream of clear liquid was pouring out of Stefan's slit. "I mean, it isn't yellow, and like I said, I don't have to do it. I don't think it's even wet, not like I'm gonna stick my fingers out and check. Now, when I jerk off, that leaves my hands sticky and wet."

"Thanks for sharing," Conner choked out.

"You really didn't know?" Stefan asked, sounding surprised. "How — well, maybe sex just isn't a big deal to old guys like you. I didn't think it was so great when I was alive, but I knew it could be. Someday I'll find someone young and hot here in our world, and we'll fall in love and fuck all the time."

"God, spare me from romantic goofballs." Conner shook his head. "You think we can fall in love?"

"Why can't we? We still have feelings."

Conner didn't have an answer for that. He glanced up at the sky, and something tugged at him. Fear settled cold in his bones—or where they'd be if he had any—and he started to panic. He wasn't sure what was happening but he didn't want to go, not up into that vast blue space, and it felt like something was trying to get him to sail up and up—

"Conner? What's going on?"

Stefan's worried voice popped Conner back to the here and now and the spot where he stood. Conner gave Stefan a mock-glare and caught him around the neck. "I'm not ancient, just old enough not to be led around by my dick," he said as he gave Stefan a noogie, rubbing his knuckles back and forth over Stefan's short hair.

"Geezer!" Stefan whooped as he jabbed at Conner's ribs. Conner had to let go before he ended up a giggling pile of goo. His ribs were very ticklish.

"You seriously didn't know about..." Stefan made a rude gesture of self-pleasure.

Conner shrugged and hoped his face wasn't red. It sure felt like it was. "I hadn't really been in the mood." *For years and years and years. Being sexually traumatised will do that to you.* Conner had never told Stefan how he'd died, and Stefan had never asked.

Stefan's eyes rounded and his mouth pursed into an 'o' before he asked, "How can you ever *not* be in the mood?"

Conner slipped, giving away more than he meant to then. "Sometimes things happen that make sex unappealing." He turned and shot up, skimming a few feet above the ground at so quick a pace that

Bailey Bradford

everything was a blur. He was too afraid to go higher, that tug from moments before still fresh in his mind.

"Where are we going?" Stefan asked.

Conner should have known he couldn't outrun the kid. He could pop off and leave Stefan, but that just seemed mean. Conner slowed down, surprised when he did to see that that went right through the other side of the town limits.

"Well, I was thinking. Where could a guy go to get laid?"

Stefan looked down, then turned those big and all too innocent eyes on him. "Um. I guess since we're both gay—"

"No." Conner felt bad when Stefan cringed. "Look, I didn't mean it bad. It's just, you're like a little brother to me. I freaked out over you whipping your dick out to…to take a fake piss!"

"It wasn't fake," Stefan grumbled. "Felt as good as when I used to do it before."

Before. I fucking hate that word. "Okay, but that's beside the point. I still think of you like the brother I never had, Stef. I can't mess around with you."

Stefan studied him closely then nodded. "I guess so. As long as it ain't 'cuz you think I'm ugly or got a little dick or anything like that."

Conner almost snorted. "That wasn't a little dick, buddy. Trust me when I tell you that, and yeah, it's just the familiarity. I refuse to admit to you being anything other than cute."

Stefan wrinkled his nose at that but grinned. "I'll take it. So what's the plan, man?"

Conner told him, and Stefan was all but bouncing in the air. "Oh, I want to go! Please? Pleasepleasepleaseplease? It's not like anyone can hurt me now, and maybe I'll find someone!"

42

"And maybe it'll be a dud of an idea," Conner said, trying to temper Stefan's excitement. He didn't want Stefan to be let down. "Seriously, I'm talking about checking out gay bars in the DFW area on the far-out hope that other dead gay men will be doing the same. You do realise that it'll probably be for nothing?"

Stefan's grin didn't dim one bit. "It'll still be fun, and if nothing else, we can ogle the hot guys, right?"

"Right," Conner said on a sigh. Even if he did find someone willing, he wouldn't be able to hook up with Stefan hanging around him. He didn't want to examine why he was kind of relieved at that, and he really didn't want to wonder if he'd have been able to get an erection thinking of anyone other than Ro. He winked at Stefan. "Looks like you got yourself a wingman."

Chapter Five

Ro knew he was spiralling out of control. He hadn't expected his mother to pass so quickly, or for her to completely abandon them in death. He was angry that she hadn't lingered like Conner, and he was angry at Conner, too, for leaving him. Ro hadn't felt the spirit's presence since that day in his bedroom. That hurt more than it should have.

His dad was lost in his own grief, and Ro's siblings had their own way of dealing with the loss, which was apparently to get the fuck out of McKinton again as fast as possible. Sev was a mess, but he had Laine, and Ro just felt lost and lonelier than ever.

The first night the truck driver had come into Virginia's Café and had told Ro he was going to fuck him until he couldn't walk, Ro had been kind of offended. He wasn't a cheap whore, but it hadn't taken much to convince him to meet the man who called himself JD in the alley after the café had closed.

Ro had been sore as hell after, JD not bothering with any more prep than donning a lubed rubber. He hadn't slowed down when Ro had asked him to, either, instead seeming turned on by the way it had hurt Ro to have that thick cock shoved into him. Ro had had bruises, too, on his hips and ass. JD had pounded into him and held him in place for it. Once JD had come, he'd reached around and jerked Ro off with painfully coarse strokes. Ro didn't even know how he'd managed to come from that, but he had.

Afterwards, he'd felt like a total slut. Even the hookups he'd had before hadn't been so seedy. He'd at least known the guy, another waiter who'd since moved on. But JD wasn't really named JD, Ro would bet on it, and he had a way about him that made Ro feel like the whore he denied being.

The next time JD had come through, Ro had refused to wait on his table. He'd had Twila take that whole section. JD had grabbed him after work, when Ro had been walking out back to his car. In retrospect, Ro should have known it would happen. JD wasn't the type to be put off, and as JD had shoved him to his knees in the alley, one big, rough hand over his mouth, Ro had known it was going to be bad. He couldn't bring himself to care. Someone was touching him, someone wanted him bad enough to not let him walk away. Ro had arched and had taken JD in eagerly then. JD hadn't been quite so forgiving of the snub from inside the café, slapping Ro's ass and thighs until they'd stung and he'd cried out against JD's hand. JD hadn't got him off then, either.

"Next time, you be good or it'll be worse," JD had told him. Ro had been so sore he hadn't been able to get up for a while. Only the sound of someone's footsteps had spurred him to move. His pants were torn and his knees were scraped and bloody. Ro didn't care. He felt used and wanted, and he'd have the proof of that on his body for a while.

Somewhere in his mind, Ro knew it was wrong, that his thinking was fucked up. Sometimes he'd even tell himself he needed help, that he was suffocating under depression and God only knew what else. But then he'd give in to the lethargy and just not do anything. He didn't have the energy or the money to get help anyway. Texas' mental health services sucked at the best of times.

His father seemed to sink deeper into a depression of his own. Ro wondered if they were feeding off each other's moods. Sev came over and Ro would put on a happy show for him, smiling and laughing and all of that, but inside he felt off, numb. Even so, he didn't want Sev feeling guilty because of it.

And Conner didn't come around. That hurt so much, more than it should have considering Conner had only popped in on him once—that he knew of. Ro sat in his bedroom one evening, after another rough fuck by JD. He took out the picture of Conner, and he felt the last bit of hope he had in him drain away.

The blond man in the picture would never be his. No one decent would, once they found out how he let JD treat him in the alley. This last time, JD had used more than his dick, pushing fingers in beside it, hurting Ro bad enough that he knew he was going to have to put a stop to the twisted thing they had going on. He was too scared to go to the doctor, couldn't imagine telling the old man what the problem was.

Ro would just have to keep an eye on it and make sure if he didn't stop bleeding that he got to the hospital no matter how embarrassing that would be. In fact, maybe he could drive into Dallas and go to a clinic there. Surely there was some place he could go and not have his family find out.

That sounded like the best plan. Ro was so sore he could hardly walk, but he gathered up his keys and quietly left the house. He got in his car and backed out of the drive. He ached, but it was the shame that truly hurt him. How had he let himself come to this point? Even as lonely as he'd been, he should have known he deserved better than to be fucked the way JD wanted. There were people who liked rough games, people who liked BDSM, but JD wasn't one of those people, and neither was Ro. JD wanted to fuck him, to hurt him, and he didn't want Ro to enjoy it at all. Ro didn't, and he wasn't going to put up with it anymore.

From here on out, he'd get his head on straight. He was worth more than what he was allowing himself to be. Ro could see now that he'd been depressed on some level for a long time. It'd kept him locked down, scared to branch out and try anything. He'd used his family as an excuse, and, while he liked McKinton well enough, staying there now would be detrimental to his health. And hell, maybe if he left, his dad would leave. Ro was afraid his father was going to die from a broken heart at the rate he was going.

Ro was making plans, finally feeling like he was breaking through the ice that'd kept him underwater. Maybe he'd had to hit rock bottom to get better. He kind of thought he had. Surely he couldn't get any lower than letting JD do the things to him that he had.

The deer surprised him, darting out in front of Ro and standing still, all big eyes and fear. "Fuck!" Ro jerked the wheel, knowing even as he did so that it was the wrong thing to do when he'd been doing seventy. The truck swerved and tyres squealed, and the last thing Ro remembered thinking was that he hoped his stupidity didn't kill his father.

Chapter Six

That tugging Conner had felt earlier was nothing
like the force that slammed into him later that night.
He and Stefan were at a club, observing the living
because his brilliant idea was a dud, when all of the
sudden, his world seemed to implode. Conner's vision
dimmed and Ro's face flashed through his mind. Not
the happy Ro or the moodier one of late, but a
terrified, screaming one that had Conner shooting
back to McKinton in a flash.

"What's wrong?" Stefan hollered, but Conner waved
him off. Stefan would be all right. He knew how to
come and go just like Conner did, and, as Stefan had
said, no one was going to hurt him now. That there
were some evil spirits as well as good ones was
something he couldn't think about right now, not
when he was certain something very bad was
happening to Ro.

If it was that fucking bastard from the alley, Conner
would tear him apart and fuck the consequences.
Conner let himself be drawn to Ro, following the

sound of his voice as it was carried across the planes of the living and the dead.

What he found made his gut twist with dread. A truck that looked very much like Ro's was crashed into a tree, the front and cab of the truck folded like an accordion from the impact.

Conner could see Ro. All the years he'd been dead, Conner hadn't experienced anything like he did then. Nausea welled up and he heaved even as he forced himself to move closer. Ro's eyes were open, and at first he thought he was too late. He howled with a grief he couldn't contain, that wasn't reasonable if he was to keep believing he felt nothing for Ro.

"Now you show up."

Quietly panted, the words tore through Conner's agony. He stopped mid-yell and blinked, looking into Ro's eyes. Could Ro see him?

"I can see you," Ro whispered brokenly. He swallowed, throat clicking and his Adam's apple bobbing. "I can see you, and you're just as handsome as always." Ro coughed, and blood frothed up around his lips. "Loved you for so long," Ro said, then his eyes dulled and his chest heaved for one rattling exhalation.

"No." Conner patted Ro's chest, fear driving him to will his hands to feel. "No, you can't die, kid. You can't!" Blood, he had blood on his hands. Ro had no pulse, no life. "No! Ro, not like this! God damn it, it'll kill Sev and your dad—"

"It's not like I did it on purpose."

"Fuck!" Conner shrieked, whirling around to find himself looking at a very sexy spirit. "Aw, hell. Ro…" Conner shook his head, torn between being sad for those Ro had left behind and relieved that Ro was there with him then.

"You're crying for me?" Ro asked, reaching out and touching him.

Conner shivered at that, feeling Ro's fingers brush over his cheek. "Why wouldn't I, Ro? You're young, you had your whole life ahead of you."

Ro cocked his head to one side and flipped back his long hair. He gave Conner a contemplative stare.

Conner found it hard to return that look, afraid that Ro would see right through him. Something selfish and awful was brewing inside him, and Conner didn't like it. He was sorry Ro was dead, but he was glad he would be able to maybe have a chance with him now. Did that make him an awful spirit?

"Whatever you're thinking, stop. It looks painful."

Conner scowled at Ro. "I'm thinking I'm a selfish bastard, because while I'm sorry you're dead, and sorry it's going to hurt so many people you left behind, now I can finally do this." Conner reached for Ro, fisting his hand in that silky black hair. Ro's eyes were about the size of saucers as Conner pulled him right up flush to him. Ro's lips parted either in surprise or invitation. Conner decided to think it was the latter as he slanted his mouth over Ro's.

Fire. Fire and honey. That was what Ro tasted like, hot and velvety and sweet. Conner groaned and licked into Ro's mouth, tasting him over and over again as he kept one hand in Ro's hair and the other on one slender hip. Ro tasted like ambrosia and every other perfect thing in existence, quenching a thirst Conner hadn't known was consuming him until then.

Ro's hands seemed to burn against him where they rested on Conner's shoulders. Conner pulled Ro closer, the fear and loss he'd felt smothering under lust and need. He canted Ro's head for a better angle and tasted every bit of Ro's mouth, memorising the texture and the sounds Ro made. Had Conner ever had a lover make such hungry noises before? He didn't think so.

Ro hitched a leg up around Conner's hip, bringing their groins together. Heat, instantaneous and radiant, flared through him. Even with his eyes closed, Conner saw swathes of red and blue—

"Dude!"

Conner jerked back from the kiss but he didn't release Ro as he slitted his eyes open enough to glare at Stefan. "What?" he rasped.

"Lights," Ro said at the same time that Stefan pointed and started babbling. "Sheriff—oh my God, Rogelio?"

Conner turned and saw that there was indeed a sheriff's car zooming up the road. He hoped to God it wasn't Laine, and it shouldn't have been because Laine had the day shift and his deputies took the night, but no.

"Fuck," he muttered, watching as Laine's familiar form shot out of the vehicle. "Aw, no. No, Laine, no…"

"What did I do?" Ro whispered. "I shouldn't have swerved, shouldn't have let JD do what he did. If I hadn't have let him hurt me—"

"Hurt you?" Conner jerked his head back around. "He hurt you?" His plan to tear JD apart was a good one.

Ro shook him by the shoulders. "I let him, so whatever you're thinking, stop it. JD didn't do anything I tried to stop him from doing." He gestured towards Laine who was running full tilt to the truck. "Can't you stop him? Don't let him see me like that."

One glance at the body Ro had left behind enough to have Conner rushing towards Laine. He didn't clothesline the man, but it was a near thing. Sometimes in his exuberance, Conner could get carried away. He was fairly desperate to keep Laine from seeing Ro, at least until he could warn him. Conner really hated to do it, but he reached for Sev, too, hoping to forewarn him of the bad news to come.

Conner hit Laine with a gust of air, his incorporeal form spreading out to block Laine's progress. It didn't faze Conner, and Laine was only stopped for a split second before he shoved back with a wave of what Conner could only think of as a psychic hit. Conner was thrown back on his butt, even if it didn't truly touch the ground. He realised then that Laine wasn't reasonable, wasn't the calm, logical man he almost always was.

And he couldn't stop Laine, couldn't protect him from this pain any more than he had been able to when he'd died.

"It's not your fault, it's mine. I shouldn't have fucking swerved." Ro bowed his head and sniffled. "God, what'd I do? Dad's going to… And Sev, and I mean, I've… I've had a crush on you forever, but this is really going to hurt my family and we just lost Mom a few months ago."

"Ro, Rogelio." Laine knocked his hat off trying to reach through the truck door. He didn't say another word then, just touched Ro's body with a trembling hand. "Shit, kid. God damn it." Laine closed Ro's eyes and rested his palm there for several long minutes, his breathing shaky and laboured. Conner saw the sheen of tears on Laine's cheeks, and he regretted trying to reach Sev, because he was pretty sure it'd worked. That would mean Sev was freaking out and maybe driving.

"I'm so sorry," Ro said, hovering beside Laine. He glanced at Conner. "Can I…? Can I touch him?"

Conner nodded. "You can try. It feels weird, but it won't hurt either of you." Laine probably wouldn't feel it at all, but Conner didn't have the time to explain to Ro how to concentrate and make himself firm enough for the living to feel his presence or touch. "Stay here, please? I need to check on Sev. I did something stupid when I saw Laine pull up, and contacted him. He's got to be panicking since all I did was tell him Laine needed him."

"Go on. I'll be here." Ro bit his lip then released it. "Right? I'm not going on to wherever?"

"You either go when you die, or you don't, as far as I've seen, so no." Conner brushed a kiss to the top of Ro's head. "Stefan, stay here with him."

"Sure thing, Con." Stefan saluted him and Conner didn't hesitate any longer. He focused on finding Sev and a split second later he was beside Sev in the car Sev was driving. Way too fast.

Conner focused on his foot and he pushed it against Sev's right calf. *"Slow down, Laine's fine. He's not hurt."* Conner wasn't lying, but he felt dishonest, so he added, *"But he does need you. Trust me when I tell you that you arriving doing ninety isn't going to help him any. Just slow down, make sure you get to him."*

That must have sounded foreboding, because Sev gasped and took his foot off the gas. "When did you become precognitive? Are you saying I'll die if I keep speeding? What the fuck do you mean?" Sev shouted the last question at him.

Conner wondered if he could get a headache. There was a pressure building right between his eyes. He pressed a thumb to it and tried to reassure Sev that he wasn't predicting a fiery death for him. Conner stayed in the car with him until Sev pulled up behind Laine's vehicle. In the distance he could hear the wail of a siren, an ambulance coming their way.

"That's Ro's truck!" Sev was out of the vehicle and running. Conner would have given anything to spare his friends this pain, but he could do nothing except be there in his spirit way.

Sev knew, before he reached the truck. Whether it was his psychic ability, or seeing his lover crying, his sobs silent and powerful, Conner didn't know. But Sev skidded to a stop and stared right at Ro where he stood with his hand resting on Laine's back.

"Ro." Sev sounded broken, there was no other word for it.

Laine turned his head the rest of the way, giving Sev more than his profile. "I'm so sorry, honey. I got here too late."

Sev moved then, joining Laine and putting his hand right where Ro's was. "No, you didn't get here too late. Did he, Ro?"

Laine blinked and took a handkerchief from his back pocket. He wiped his face and pulled Sev to him. "He's here?"

"With Conner and Stefan," Sev confirmed. "It doesn't help. I thought it would, if Alma stayed after she passed away, but now I know it wouldn't have mattered. It still fucking hurts."

"I shouldn't have swerved," Ro said again.

Conner touched his cheek. Ro looked at him and Conner knew he had to be the biggest jerk in the world, because every second he was with Ro, he was more and more glad Ro was there. Which meant he was glad Ro was dead, but he wasn't, but—

"Stop thinking so hard," Ro told him.

"Stop thinking about what you should or shouldn't have done," Conner retorted. "Take it from someone who knows. I've had years and years of the afterlife to learn that thinking about what you could have done different only makes you crazy."

Ro nibbled on his bottom lip again as he watched Sev and Laine. "I can't help it. I've hurt them, and my dad. God help him, please." Ro tilted his head up and closed his eyes. "If You're up there, please, please help my dad. Help him through this." Ro lowered his head again and turned his dark eyes on Conner. "I don't think I'm everything in Dad's world, but my brother and sister aren't around much, and with Mom having passed away, I'm worried about him. Sev told me Mom went on. Do you know what's after this?"

"No, and I don't want to." That would be like another death for him. "I think we stay here as long as we want to, maybe. Others go wherever there is to go other than here." But there'd been that tug... Conner wasn't going to think about that. "Where'd Stefan go?"

"I don't know." Ro looked at Sev and Laine. "Sev, can you hear me?"

"It takes practice—" Conner started, because it had taken him years to be able to reach a living human being. But Sev stood straighter and spun to look right at Ro.

"Ro?" Sev's tears shone under the moonlight. Laine turned and his gaze landed on Ro as well. Sev moved a step forward then held out his hand. "Ro? What happened?"

Ro cocked his head and glanced at Conner, who surely didn't know what to think, then at Sev. "Deer. I swerved, even though you, Laine and Dad always told me not to. I should have listened, but I was distracted."

"Were you texting?" Laine asked, then his eyes about bugged out of his head. "How'd I hear you? Sev? Sev, how'd I hear him?" Laine clutched Sev's shoulders and pulled Sev against him. "I don't have psychic abilities."

"No, you don't." Sev frowned, pulling up a deep line across his forehead. "But maybe Ro does."

"Me?" Ro thumped his own chest. "I don't."

"I think you do," Sev argued. "Laine can hear you. That isn't him, that's you. Conner had to work really hard to communicate with me. Even now, sometimes it's a struggle for him. He's great at making parts of himself corporeal, and at tormenting people, but you I can hear clearly."

Ro went back to biting his lip and Conner's dick thought that was a fine time to plump up. He was damned glad Sev and Laine couldn't see him. They'd both want to wallop him.

"Laine, you can hear me?" Ro finally asked.

Laine's expression was almost comical. Would have been, Conner thought, if he didn't still have tears streaming down his cheeks.

"Yeah, kid, I can." Laine let go of Sev then and held out his hand. The question was unspoken, but Ro understood it. He reached for Laine.

"Concentrate. Think about making your hand firm, dense, so he can feel it," Conner advised.

Ro laid his hand in Laine's, and at first Laine didn't seem to notice. Then he gasped and curled his fingers around Ro's.

"Oh." Laine smiled tremulously and cupped the top of Ro's hand with his other one. "Rogelio, I'm sorry you passed, but I'm glad of this, that we have this at least."

"I said it didn't help, but somehow, with Laine being able to hear you too, I can't help but feel—" Sev stopped and muttered something Conner didn't catch. "Well, shit. There's no right way to say it, but I feel better now. It's like you're not gone at all. Except I won't see you again." Sev burst into tears again and Laine let go of Ro to embrace Sev while he cried.

"Come on, let's give them some privacy." Probably a weird thing for him to say, but Conner meant it. He took Ro's hand. "Let me show you how this is done." Conner whisked Ro away, leaving Sev and Laine to comfort one another.

Chapter Seven

The stoic way his dad took the news was worse even than if he'd have broken down. Ro tried to reach out to Roger, but there was some sort of barrier that seemed to be erected around him. Ro bounced right off it and collided with Conner. Conner frowned and tried to pass the barrier too but his hand ended up pressed flat against the air like it was touching a window or a wall.

Sev and Laine were with Roger, and Ro didn't want to interrupt as they were explaining to him what had happened. It hurt Ro that his dad didn't ask if he'd passed on.

"I think he's in shock," Conner said, tucking Ro to his side. "Maybe that's why he seems so cold."

Ro didn't have anything to say to that. His dad had loved him, and his behaviour now confused Ro. "I guess I'm being childish, wanting him to mourn. That's horrible, but I feel like he doesn't care at all."

Conner jostled him slightly and scolded, "You know better. There's only so much a person can take before they break, and I think your dad is at that point. I watched Roger and Alma raise you and your brother and sister. I know how much they both love their kids. This, with your dad, is his mind trying to keep him from shattering."

"I shouldn't—" Ro began.

"No, don't go there. I told you it's not going to do you a bit of good." Conner made a gesture with one hand and Sev's hair rippled. Sev slanted a look their way and Conner sent him a message, letting Sev know they were going to leave. "He'll tell your dad, when the time is right."

"I hope so," Ro said, letting Conner whisk him out of the house. "I hate that Dad's hurting so bad, I hate that he's keeping me out. Do you think he's doing it on purpose?"

"I don't know. I never approached Roger or your mom since they seemed a little uncomfortable or maybe superstitious about me." Conner had them in the air, soaring through the darkness. Ro might actually have enjoyed it had he not been so confused by everything that had happened and guilt-laden over hurting his dad.

"Where are we going?" he asked after a minute of silence.

Conner rolled them until they were on their sides, slipping through the night sky. His eyes shone with bright flecks of white, reflecting the moonlight. Ro forgot his first question for another one.

"How is that possible? How can I see the moon reflecting in your eyes? Why am I wearing clothes?" He glanced down his body then back at Conner. "And they aren't even the clothes I was wearing when I wrecked!" Could spirits have panic attacks? Ro's heart was slamming against his ribs—"Do I have a heart? Conner, what the hell are we?"

Conner lowered them to the ground, not that Ro felt it. In fact, it seemed as if they were still in the air. Before Ro could freak out over anything else, Conner put one of his big hands on Ro's nape again and the other on his hip. Ro's mouth was parted on a question he was forming when Conner lowered his mouth to Ro's for a kiss that zinged fiery need straight to Ro's cock.

Ro's panic and confusion was eradicated by the plundering of his mouth. Conner kissed him with a need Ro had never experienced before. He was breathless, panting and shaking, when Conner raised his head enough to murmur against his lips.

"We have form and substance, to other spirits naturally and to humans in small measure when we concentrate hard enough. You can see the moon in my eyes like I can see the want in yours because we exist, and we *are*." Conner kissed him again, ending it with a sucking nip to Ro's bottom lip. "Whether we feel our hearts beat from some sort of memory, or whether it's really in there with us, does it matter? Or is it more important that we just feel?"

Ro shook his head slightly, dazed by the strength of the arousal he was experiencing. "Can we —?" He looked over the man he'd built his teenage fantasies around. Conner was every bit as big and handsome in this form as he'd been in life. His shoulders were almost twice the width of Ro's, and he had deep dimples that dented his cheeks when he smiled. Ro hadn't seen that in the picture, which had been of a more professional standard. Conner had been in his fireman's uniform, and his smile had been more of a smirk.

"Can we what?" Conner asked, dragging his teeth along the side of Ro's neck.

Ro shivered and rubbed his aching erection against one of Conner's thighs. He told himself shyness was stupid here in their afterlife. He'd bypassed so many opportunities when he'd been alive and wasn't going to do the same thing now. "Can we fuck?"

Conner snapped his head back, and those blue eyes of his were positively huge as he gawped at Ro.

Ro tilted his head to the side and watched a faint blush rise to Conner's cheeks. A check of Conner's groin showed him to be sporting a large bulge. Ro ran his hands down to cup that hot length. Conner filled both hands with a steely cock that made Ro want to beg to be fucked.

"Can we?" he asked again, stroking that tempting shaft.

Conner gasped, and gripped him tighter, pulling Ro's hair and bruising—if he could bruise—Ro's hip. A shudder racked the bigger man as a moan tore past his lips. Ro felt the pulse of Conner's cock right before wet warmth spread from the tip.

Amused and flattered at how quickly Conner had shot, Ro winked at him. "I take that as a yes?"

"Oh God," Conner whined as he slapped a hand to his forehead. "I'm gonna just go die again."

Ro didn't think that was funny. In fact, part of his need was to escape the thoughts of what had happened to him. A larger part, however, was that he finally could touch the man he'd wanted for so very long.

"Hey, don't be embarrassed. I'm flattered." Ro caught Conner's hand before he could smack himself again. He tugged that big paw down and pressed it against his own dick. "And really, really horny. Conner." Ro humped Conner's hand, need coiling in his gut. "I don't want to think. Help me forget, at least for a little while."

Conner gulped and Ro wondered why he seemed so scared. Conner filled him in right quick. "I haven't, uh." Conner squeezed Ro's cock and moaned softly, his eyelids drooping nearly shut. "Not since before I was killed."

Ro was almost too lost in how good it felt to be touched. He was rutting away, pleasure building in his balls with each thrust, when Conner's words sank in. Ro stilled and did some quick math. "Over twenty years, Conner?" he blurted out. Jesus, no wonder Conner had gone off like a lit firecracker.

"Don't laugh at me," Conner huffed, sounding hurt.

Ro practically climbed up the man, wrapping his legs around Conner's narrow hips and his arms around his thick neck. "I wouldn't. I'm not. That's just a long time."

"Time is…different, here," Conner muttered. "I swear yesterday Laine and Sev were young and just freshly in love, and now they're almost old."

Ro snorted and when he inhaled, he caught the most delicious scent of musk and man. "You smell so good." He forgot about his intentions of telling Conner Sev and Laine would shit bricks over the old comment. He forgot about everything but the need pulsing in his groin, the scent and taste of Conner's skin as he nibbled under Conner's jaw.

"Ungh." Conner gripped his ass, squeezing it firmly, and Ro murmured encouragement as he kept sampling Conner's jaw, licking and sucking it. There was the slight rasp of stubble against his tongue, and it ratcheted up Ro's arousal. He'd always wanted Conner, always, and now he could finally have him.

"Did you mean it?" Conner asked him, something very close to longing in his voice, Ro thought.

"Did I mean—" Ro had a flash then, a bright and embarrassing moment of his confession to Conner. "Uh." God, how did he answer that without being an asshole?

Conner's hands stilled on his backside as Conner looked away. The moonlight painted his profile silver and grey, accentuating the cut of Conner's cheekbone. "It's okay. I shouldn't have brought it up. You were scared and—"

"Conner." Ro framed Conner's face in his hands, turning that handsome man's gaze back on him. "I don't know about love, because I don't know you, not really. But I've had a crush on you for half my life." He huffed and rolled his eyes. "Well, and now, too. You're... Look, I compared every man I met to you, you know. I wanted you to come visit me like you did Laine and Sev, wanted your attention. You never gave it to me, then... Then you did, and I hoped... But I didn't see you again. I thought you were mad at me for snooping or something, and it hurt." Ro laughed at how ridiculous he sounded, like a kid instead of a man.

"It's all right. I just haven't had anyone tell me that and I thought you were just babbling anyway."

But Ro could tell Conner was disappointed.

"I wasn't mad at you, either," Conner continued. "I mean, seeing that stuff, yeah it bothered me, but not because I was mad at you. I didn't want you looking at those articles and pitying me. The fact is, except for my death, I had a really good life."

Ro arched a brow at Conner. "Well, I would think that the death part would never be good. I didn't enjoy it." He barely repressed a shudder. "I felt like every nerve ending in my body was throbbing with agony, then it just quit, and you were there, and I died."

Conner tipped his chin and began caressing Ro's butt again. "Yeah, but it took me several hours to die, Ro. I'm not saying it was less painful for you, but the time it was dragged out—I don't like thinking about that, or remembering when Laine found me. That was even worse almost than being carved up. My life until then was good, though. I wish I'd been brave enough to come out, but I wasn't, and if I had been, I would have lost Laine sooner, or never even had him."

"Why did you stay away from me then?" Ro asked.

"Because I was ashamed. I thought, here's this man I've watched grow from a cute, awkward teenager into this sexy, sleek guy." Conner smiled a little, one side of his mouth tipping higher than the other. "I tried not to think about you, but for the first time in ages, I got hard. I wanted you, but what was the point to that?" Conner shrugged. "Looking at the picture of me you had, there was just a lot of things that hit me. Then your mother passed away, and she went right up. I knew I didn't want to go where she went. I wasn't—" Conner stopped, took a deep breath then let it go. "I'm *not* ready to go anywhere. I want to be right here, watching over my friends, the people I love, even if it hurts to see them growing old, to know they'll die and I may not ever see them again then."

Conner brought one hand up to cup Ro's chin. "And it hurt like a mother to find you being fucked by some guy in the alley."

Ro had thought he'd felt like a slut before, but hearing that Conner had seen him letting JD use him was absolutely mortifying. He squirmed and tried to wiggle free. Ro wished he knew how to make himself disappear. Surely spirits could do that. All he wanted was to hide away, like in a closet or attic somewhere.

"Fuck!" he yelped as he went from looking at Conner's neck and chin to total darkness. "Fuck, what'd I do?" *Don't panic, don't panic! I'm a damn ghost, spirit – whatever! What could possibly hurt me now?*

Despite that logic, Ro was in full freak-out mode seconds later. He couldn't see, everything was black, so black his eyeballs ached from straining to pick out even a hint of where he was. The air was hot around him, and, even though he knew intellectually that he couldn't suffocate, his body—corporeal or not—hadn't got the memo.

Ro kicked and slapped at the darkness. He thought he touched something but it wasn't firm enough to give resistance so he figured he was imagining it. He tried to yell, but fear clawed at his throat, then bands of steel were around his waist and the scream tore free—but it didn't make a sound.

Chapter Eight

"It's just me, Ro, it's just me," Conner said quietly into Ro's ear as he kissed the curve of it. "Ro, it's okay."

"Can't breathe," Ro rasped out.

Conner started to argue that but decided it'd just be quicker to remove them from the small enclosure. When Ro had popped away from him, Conner had been astounded. It'd taken him a while to learn that trick. Then it dawned on him that Ro probably didn't *know* that trick, and most likely was freaking the fuck out because he'd just vanished and reappeared somewhere else.

It had only taken him seconds to concentrate and locate Ro's position. Leave it to Ro to have zapped himself into Sev's attic. Dusty, dark and hotter than hell, it'd give anyone fits. If Ro hadn't panicked, he might have recognised where he was, but he had panicked, and now Conner had his arms full of clingy, sexy man again.

Conner took them both to an open meadow made into an almost magical-looking place by the moonlight. He laid them atop the swaying grass, willing them to have some weight so that the tall strands bent under them.

Ro wouldn't look at him, just held onto Conner and buried his face in Conner's chest. Conner didn't want Ro to be ashamed. All he'd done was have sex with someone. It wasn't like Conner hadn't done the same with anonymous men before he'd hooked up with Laine. It was stupid of him to get his undies in a knot because Ro had sought out an escape from his pain with another man. *Then. Now, he's mine.* Conner didn't think Ro would mind, either.

Conner tipped Ro's chin up, having to tug a little harder than he'd hoped to get Ro to meet his gaze. When he did, Conner spoke. "I don't care who you've been with. It doesn't matter now. This is a new start for us. It embarrassed me to admit that I hadn't bothered to get off in so long. I honestly had no desire, until I looked at you one day." Conner forced himself to continue, pushing past his discomfort at making himself vulnerable. "I saw you, it was after your twenty-first birthday, maybe a year or two later. I'm bad with time." He gave Ro a kiss on the tip of his pert nose. "I remember thinking you'd grown into yourself and admiring your determination to stay in McKinton with your family when they needed you. Not many children do that once they grow up. They just leave their parents behind and go on with their lives, you know. Then I noticed how attractive you were, the way your hair glinted under the light in your room, or the way the wind lifted it and spread it out behind you."

Conner dipped his head and took another kiss, this one from Ro's parted lips. He sighed afterwards and smoothed a hand down to cup Ro's butt. "I knew there was something about you, something that fascinated me and soothed me at the same time that it stirred me up. I wasn't ready to think about sex, not when it came to myself, though. Understand, the fucker who killed me, he beat off while he did it. More than once." Conner couldn't repress the sick feeling it gave him still.

Ro gasped before sucking his lips in, sealing them tight. Then he opened his mouth and licked those swollen lips as he pressed a hand over Conner's heart. "I'm sorry. I didn't know. It didn't mention it in the reports I read. I didn't mean to make light of it before, when you, uh, came."

"It wasn't in the reports because he came into his handkerchief, and I guess he burned it or something. I don't know because he was doing it again when I died." Conner's stomach turned, and if he'd thought it would have helped purge the memory, he'd have rolled on over and puked. Time had taught him that such an easy riddance wasn't possible, so he kept talking past the tensing and rolling of his belly. "I never told Sev. I didn't want anyone to know." Conner looked in Ro's dark eyes, so big and framed with such thick long lashes he could happily lose himself in the depths of those peepers. "I understand feeling dirty, Ro. Somehow, him doing that was worse than him killing me. It made me feel less human, less valuable, like a cum dump for the sick fucker. And that's how I died, feeling hurt and nasty."

"Conner," Ro began, only to stop and sob quietly. He nestled right against Conner, stroking Conner from thigh to shoulder then back down, over and over until a tension Conner hadn't been aware of left his body, loosening his muscles and taking with it the anger and shame that had cropped up in him.

It was enough—Ro's touch and that relief from emotions he didn't want to feel. Conner leaned over and pushed Ro onto his back, Ro's arms going around his neck to embrace him as he lowered his mouth to Ro's.

The slick warmth and sweet taste of Ro zinged through Conner, settling firmly in his groin. His cock sprang up, hard and eager, his balls drawing tight to his body.

Oh no you don't. Not again. I'll last long enough to make love to Ro one way or another. He grabbed his cock at the base, squeezing firmly. When that didn't help, he added a pinch. Pain flared but he got himself under control. Conner rubbed his hand up, over Ro's flat belly, over his ribs, willing Ro's clothes away as he went. It didn't take more than a thought for Conner to be naked as well, then it was fire and need as they were skin on skin, their incorporeal forms every bit as sensitive to each other's touch as living beings would have been to one another.

Ro's body was exquisite, felt exquisite beneath Conner's larger one. Conner pinched a nipple at the same time that he sucked on Ro's tongue. Ro arched and moaned for him. Ro's cock poked at Conner's thigh. Conner felt the pre-cum leaking from Ro's tip, smelt it in the air.

"Fuck," he rasped as he dragged his lips along Ro's jaw to his neck. He sucked the tender spot under Ro's ear as Ro undulated and panted beneath him. Ro grabbed Conner's ass with both hands and pulled, urging him forward, parting Conner's cheeks and exposing his hole to the night breeze. Whether Conner really felt it or only imagined it didn't matter. It was as factual a sensation in his brain as any other erotic experience had ever been.

Conner rolled them over, putting Ro on top then, because a memory sparked in his mind, one of him and Laine. It wasn't a turn-on, more of a warning from his subconscious, he figured, reminding him that even when he'd been alive, he'd been the one getting fucked. Laine had always topped, and Conner wasn't sure he could trust himself to go slow if he tried to take Ro now.

Ro raised his head, confusion puckering his brow. "You want me to ride you?"

Conner shook his head even as his cock twitched at that idea. "No, I want you to fuck me. It's been a while, remember?" He decided he had to risk being tacky when Ro gave him an exasperated look. "Longer even, because I didn't top, not with Laine."

Ro jerked back a little at that. "I don't—I've never topped, Conner. I'd rather have you in me this time. Please?"

Conner started to argue and Ro reached behind himself, doing something that Conner couldn't see.

"I told you, I was hurt," Ro said after a moment. "But I'm not now, and I don't want that...time to be in my mind, to have any power over me."

Like Conner's last memory had held him prisoner for so long. Conner got it.

Ro blanched and scrabbled to sit on him, peppering Conner's face with kisses. "Crap, I didn't mean anything bad, I just know how I am. I'll wallow, like I had been for months since Mom passed away."

Conner caught a handful of Ro's hair and began winding it in his fist. He cupped a round, soft butt cheek with his other hand. His fingers brushed over Ro's pucker and Ro froze before moaning. They'd talked enough, he thought.

When he kissed Ro again, Conner put every bit of his need into it. Years of pent-up and ignored desire flowed from him as he hungrily claimed Ro's mouth. Ro whimpered and clutched at his shoulders, then rocked so that Conner flipped them over again, pinning Ro beneath him.

Conner thumbed Ro's jaw, pushing his head back. It exposed more of Ro's long neck and Conner took advantage immediately. Possessiveness soared through him as he saw that even in this form, he left marks on Ro's skin, purple love bites that he hoped remained for days. He worked his way down to Ro's collarbone, nibbling and dotting Ro's body with hickies.

Ro panted for him, cursed and urged him on. When Ro stared begging and tried to reach for his own cock, Conner caught his wrist and pulled Ro's hand up to hold it above Ro's shoulder. "Leave it there unless you're gonna touch me."

Ro immediately buried his fingers in Conner's hair. "Please. Fuck, God, please, Conner!"

Conner licked his way to one dark, taut nipple. It looked almost black in the night, like rich dark chocolate. Conner nipped it first, and Ro groaned, holding his head there as if demanding more.

The bittersweet taste of Ro's skin was the strongest aphrodisiac. Conner straddled Ro's body, planting a knee between Ro's legs, right up against Ro's balls. His other knee was beside Ro's left hip. Ro began rubbing and humping away as Conner worked his tit into a hot, swollen peak.

Then Conner went after the other one. He used his hands to trace patterns down Ro's sides, up to his neck then over his biceps to his forearms. Back and forth Conner went as he loved on Ro's nipples. When he was satisfied and Ro was begging him for more, Conner reached down and palmed Ro's balls. They were snug in their sac, pressed close to Ro's body.

"You gonna be able to wait until I'm in you?" Conner asked, forcing the words past his lust-dried throat.

"If you hurry," Ro gritted out. "Hurry!"

Conner looked at the long, thick length of Ro's dick. He wanted to taste it, to try to take it all the way into his throat, but he'd have to wait. Ro wanted him in a different way, and Conner was going to see to it that Ro got what he needed. Conner manoeuvred himself into a better position, kneeling between Ro's thighs, then he slid down onto his belly. He got his hands beneath Ro's ass and pushed. Ro grabbed the backs of his legs and pulled them up, raising his hips and spreading his ass for Conner.

"I don't have lube, but…" Conner used his thumbs to spread Ro open more, then he licked over the tight little swirl nestled between Ro's cheeks. "Oh, oh hell." Fuck, he'd missed this, how had he not realised? Conner dived in, rimming Ro like he was starving for it, sucking and laving that little hole until it was wet and gaping, slicked with saliva and almost ready for him.

Conner sucked two fingers, coating them well before letting off and pushing them slowly into Ro's pucker. The velvet warmth of the man, the way his ring clenched and his inner walls rippled around Conner's fingers, was almost too much. The need to be inside Ro was like a weight pressing down on Conner, threatening to steal his breath unless he hurried.

Hurting Ro wasn't going to happen, though, not in any way. Conner rotated his wrist, stretching Ro's guardian muscle, preparing him for what was likely to be a short, hard ride.

"Please," Ro gasped. "Fuck me already, Conner. In me."

Conner gritted his teeth, telling himself to hold on another minute. He found the little nub inside Ro, rubbed over it gently.

"Ah!" Ro twisted on his fingers, shoving his butt down. He wailed and pinched his own nipples as Conner watched. That broke Conner's restraint, and he pulled his fingers out. He lapped at Ro's pucker a few more times, getting it as wet as he could, then he slicked his own shaft with saliva.

"Look at me," he ordered.

Ro opened his eyes and took a hold of his knees again, pulling them clear up to his ears just about. Conner lined his cock up, letting the tip touch Ro's opening. "Keep them open," he whispered, "please." *See me. Let me see you.*

As if he heard Conner's thought, Ro nodded. "Yes."

Conner braced a hand where he'd placed Ro's earlier, above Ro's shoulder. He canted his hips and hissed as the crown of his cock sank into Ro, stretching that wet pucker around it.

Conner had to fight to keep his own eyes open at the incomparable pleasure that filled him from toes to the top of his skull. It made him tingle all down his spine, over his own hole and down to his balls. An incoherent sound spilled from his lips as Ro's body just sucked his cock right in, massaging and milking his length.

"Fuck yes," Ro chanted, "fuck yes, fuck yes," until it was almost a song in Conner's ears. He lowered himself to his elbows and pushed his arms under Ro's shoulders so he could get his hands into the long, dark hair. Then Conner slanted his mouth to Ro's, having to hunch to do so because of their height difference, but it was worth it to be able to kiss Ro as he sank the last few inches of his dick into Ro's tight ass. He closed his eyes and let himself go in the delicious sensations Ro brought to him.

Ro shook so hard beneath him Conner thought he might come apart. Then Conner couldn't think at all because Ro's inner walls contracted around his dick, driving everything but the need for release out of Conner's mind.

Conner pulled out halfway then thrust back in. He grunted, unable to form words as ecstasy stole his ability to do anything but mate with this one man. He was dimly aware of Ro holding onto him, of the sharp bite of Ro's fingernails scoring his biceps, but Conner could dwell on it.

He was melting from the inside out as Ro's body welcomed him eagerly over and over. Conner felt more animal than man, his baser nature taking over as he got to his knees, sliding them up until he was almost folding Ro in half. Guttural sounds were torn from him and Ro both as Conner pushed into Ro's ass. Ro drove his hips up, eager for each thrust, and he whined and keened every time Conner withdrew even an inch.

Conner tried to hold back, some inner voice nagging him to wait, *wait,* but it wasn't until he opened his eyes and saw Ro try to reach between them that a brain cell flared to life and it occurred to him what he was waiting for. Conner growled and caught Ro's wrist again.

"Mine," he got out right before he levered himself up enough to get his hand on Ro's dick. It was hot and hard and leaking pre-cum. Conner pumped it once, twice, then Ro's sweet mouth opened on a shriek that would have done a banshee proud. His ass clamped down on Conner's shaft, and spunk shot from Ro's slit in hot white spurts.

Conner's eyes crossed, his vision blurring and doubling and doing all sorts of new tricks. He pushed in as deep as he could and his cock pulsed, releasing his seed into Ro's body. His earlier climax had seemed explosive at the time, but it was nothing compared to this, to marking Ro inside with his very essence.

"Give it to me," Ro whispered just before the last jet of cum spurted from Conner's dick. He squeezed his butt and Conner yelped in surprise as another dribble of jizz left him. Conner collapsed on Ro but had enough sense to will his body to be more fluff than not. Ro wrapped his arms around Conner and held him tightly.

"That was worth dying for," Ro said after a while.

Conner raised his head and glared. "That's not funny, Rogelio." Even if he agreed, on his part at least. "You had—"

"I had nothing," Ro said, anger giving his voice an edge. "Don't tell me I did. I was too scared to do anything other than wait tables at Virginia's Café. I wasn't close to my siblings anymore. I was depressed and angry and Dad doesn't seem like he's going to miss me—"

"You had more than you realised," Conner corrected, wishing he could make Ro understand. "A lot of people loved you, and will miss you." But Conner stopped there, because the fact was, he loved Ro, too, and now he didn't have to lie to himself about it.

Chapter Nine

It was never a good thing to wake because you felt like you were being watched. Ro didn't handle it well at all, screeching when his eyes popped open and he found a blurry face too close to his own.

"Ack!" someone yelped.

Ro flailed his arms, smacking into something, and he blinked in time to see Stefan fly backwards as if hit by an invisible hoof to the gut. Conner appeared then, looking perplexed before he burst into raucous laughter. Ro didn't think anything was funny when he first woke up. He'd never been a morning person, and that didn't seem likely to change now.

Conner was still chortling, him and Stefan both now. Ro stood up then quickly let out a mortified sound when he realised he was bare-assed naked.

"Just think on your clothes, man," Stefan advised around giggles. He got himself together while Ro closed his eyes and pictured himself wearing his most comfortable outfit. Stefan must have taken his acquiescence as a need to hear more, because he started talking as Ro willed himself to be clothed.

"You expected to be naked so you are. Just like you expected to have to sleep, so you did. Man, once I realised I never had to sleep again, I was bummed and happy both. Bummed because sleep is so good sometimes, but happy because there's so much I could be doing instead of snoozing!"

"Enthusiastic, ain't he?" Conner asked, his lips brushing against Ro's ear.

Ro opened his eyes and was relieved to find Stefan had been right and his dangly bits were no longer dangling quite so freely. "He's helpful." Ro smoothed a wrinkle out of his shirt then asked Conner, "Where were you?"

Conner looked away and sighed. "Went to check on everyone. That weird-ass wall is still around your dad. I tried talking to Sev but he shooed me off because he was talking with the funeral parlour guy."

"Well, that's not depressing," Ro muttered, reminded again that he'd only just died and had left people behind to hurt. "I feel so scattered, like I should be more shook up, more freaked out, I don't know."

Conner turned back to him then and pulled him in for a hug. "It took me a lot longer than it's taken you to get to where you are. Honestly, right after I died, I don't even think I was whole, if that makes any sense."

"I was scared and confused," Stefan said before Ro could ask what Conner meant. "I was still pretty stupid back then."

"Stefan!" Conner snapped. "Don't talk about yourself like that, not even in the past tense. You were never stupid."

Stefan rolled his eyes so hard Ro was surprised they didn't hear the tendons straining. "Riiiiiiiiight. I was" —Stefan hooked two fingers from each hand in the air—"intellectually challenged. Whatever."

"You can be sit-challenged," Conner warned.

"What the hell does that mean?" Ro asked.

Stefan sniffed and turned his nose up at them. "It means Conner will try to paddle my behind. He'd have to catch me first, though, and he's *old*!"

"Brat." Conner growled the word and Stefan giggled then vanished, off to tease someone else, Ro was sure.

"What did you mean when you said you didn't think you were whole after you first passed?" he asked Conner then.

Conner steered them over to a shady patch of grass beneath a huge old oak tree. They sat, Ro not feeling the ground beneath him but that was okay. He was more interested in Conner's explanation than he was in anything else. Conner didn't keep him waiting.

"The thing is, I don't know how we come to be like this, what makes us stay, but I figure our brains work on electrical impulses, or have some kind of electrical current."

Ro nodded, following along so far.

Conner linked their hands together and continued, "Okay, well, I don't know how that works, but it seems like all those electric particles have to keep going on when the body doesn't, you know? Like that energy has to go somewhere, and I could be way wrong, but I prefer to believe that's us, the core of us, our soul or whatever you want to call it." Conner tilted his chin towards the sky. "Like water, how it evaporates then comes back down to Earth as rain. I know it's all more complicated than that, but maybe it's as simple as that kind of recycling, too."

"It sounds as likely as anything else," Ro said after thinking about it. "So how were you not whole?"

"I'm not sure, I just felt like I was scattered, like someone took all those protons and neutrons, whatever it was that had a current running through me, and tossed them up like a handful of confetti. Pieces of me were everywhere." Conner squeezed his hands. "I didn't come to like you did, passing over from life to death and retaining everything about myself. I remember some things, but it took me a while to feel like I had any substance. At first I was terrified and hurting still." He shrugged. "Maybe it was the trauma of how I died. Don't suppose there's anything saying a spirit can't suffer from that."

How anyone wouldn't be haunted by such a violent death was beyond Ro. "Makes sense. So what happened?"

Conner drew them back until they were lying, looking up at the green canopy of leaves. Ro didn't think they were nearly as fascinating as the man beside him, so he chose to watch Conner instead. "What happened was, I became aware in fits and starts, and somehow gathered myself together, kinda like a magnet taking up metal shavings. Then one day, it was just right, done. I was as whole as I'd ever be, and things began to snap together in my head, the need to reach Laine the most pressing. Took me over three years, but I did it. Now, here I am."

"Here we are," Ro corrected.

"Yeah, that too," Conner agreed, his lips curling up in a smile that brought out those dimples.

Ro wondered if he should suggest they get up. There were things he needed to do, like check on his dad and learn how to be a proper spirit—or at least how to do that popping in and out thing. But Ro didn't want to think about any of that now. He wanted to stay there beside Conner, studying that chiselled profile for at least a week.

What did he really have to do? Ro thought about it. He didn't want to go to the funeral home—that was more than he felt capable of handling. Seeing his own body hadn't fazed him last night, but he'd been confused and discombobulated. Today, however, he cringed just thinking about seeing his corpse. Checking in on his dad was something he did need to take care of. Even though Conner had said Roger was still walled off from them being able to get too close, Ro still wanted to see him for himself.

"Can we go see Dad?"

"We can do whatever you want to." Conner ran a hand through his thick blond hair, pulling the ends of it at his crown before letting go. "Adela and Martin are with him, or they were when I checked on Roger a few minutes ago."

"So he's not alone." A knot of worry in his chest loosened a little knowing that his sister and brother were there. He didn't feel as pressing a need to go now that he knew his da wasn't alone. "How were they?"

Conner startled him by lifting him and settling Ro between his legs. With an arm around his middle, Conner pulled Ro until his back was pressed to Conner's chest. It felt good, right. Safe, though Ro didn't know what he might be unsafe from at this point.

"They were sad, Ro, I'm not going to lie to you." Conner kissed the side of his head, his ear, down to his neck where he inhaled, rubbing his nose on Ro's skin. "You smell so good."

Ro's cock perked up but he twisted his head around to frown at Conner. "Are you trying to distract me?"

Conner grinned crookedly, making Ro's heart flutter. "Maybe. Sometimes you have to let the living grieve and give them a little time. I learnt that from popping in on people more than I should have."

Ro frowned harder, until his forehead kind of ached with it. "What would I be hurting, going in and checking on him?" Conner licked his lips and glanced away. The man was sexy as fuck but Ro wasn't going to be put off. He had the distinct impression Conner knew something he didn't. "Where did you go earlier? Just to see how my dad was?"

"I went to see Laine, too." Conner still wouldn't look at him, and for the first time, Ro wondered if Conner was still in love with Laine, if there was something going on between the two. He didn't think Laine would ever cheat on Sev, but if it was with a spirit, would it count?

"Rogelio, I don't know where your mind went to but get it out of there, because that ain't good thoughts you're having."

Ro squirmed and moved until he had himself turned around, kneeling and facing Conner. "Are you still in love with Laine?" Even asking made him want to cry, a stupid reaction for a man his age, but he'd wanted Conner for so long—

"I'll always love him," Conner said slowly, caution clear in his pretty blue eyes. "But not like *that* kind of love, Ro. I don't pine after him anymore, or fantasise that he's mine." Conner's cheeks went ruddy and he looked down at his hands, folded on his belly. "I won't lie and say I didn't do that for some time, because I sure enough did. Even after he and Sev fell in love, sometimes I'd let myself imagine me and Laine together again, in life or in death. But…"

Conner raised his gaze back to Ro's. "But one morning I peeked in on them, and they were making love."

He smiled cheekily, looking for all the world like a mischievous kid. "I've never had an issue with how nosy I am, and Laine and Sev didn't really seem to mind most of the time. Usually I'd goose one of them or throw sheets over them, just mess with them and throw 'em off stride."

Ro wasn't sure what to make of that. He had no desire to see Laine and Sev having sex. The very thought of it made him shudder.

"Well it probably grosses you out because they're your family," Conner said, having obviously figured out Ro's ick factor with the whole thing. "But they aren't mine, and I've always been a prankster. But anyway, I stayed hovering, stunned by the way Laine was touching Sev. There was such…" Conner hummed for a second then nodded. "Reverence, that's the word. Laine touched Sev with such reverence, like he was the most precious thing in the world. And Sev was the same way with Laine. It was beautiful, and I learnt then that I could still cry, that my heart could break even though I was so happy for them both. That's when I stopped letting my loneliness dictate my behaviour so much."

"I've seen them touch and look at each other like there's no one else in the world," Ro said, scooting closer to Conner. "My parents were like that. I don't think I ever heard either of them ever say a truly harsh word to the other. They didn't let Mom's parents divide them when it came down to the nitty-gritty. Instead they brought us here, to McKinton, and raised us away from the toxic people we'd been around before then."

"You ever heard from your grandparents on your mom's side, or any of your aunts and uncles in San Antonio?"

"No." And Ro didn't care to. That side of the family had disowned Sev for being gay, for being psychic — just for not being someone they could control. When Alma had taken a stand as well, her parents had reacted with hate and that was something Ro couldn't forget. "My family is here, in McKinton, and wherever Adela and Martin are. We aren't as close as we used to be, but that doesn't mean we don't love each other. We just have different lives — I mean — "

Conner stopped him from babbling by leaning forward and brushing a soft kiss over Ro's lips. "I know what you mean."

Ro moved closer, chasing Conner's lips when Conner sat back again, but Conner stopped him with a gentle hand to his chest. "Are you done asking questions about where I was?"

How the hell was he supposed to think with Conner touching him? Ro took a moment to gather his thoughts then he rocked back onto his heels. "Why don't you just tell me?"

Conner hitched up a shoulder and winked at him. "Thought you were enjoying grilling me."

Was Conner trying to distract him? Was he hiding something from Ro? It seemed best to just ask and be direct. "Where were you, and are you trying to mess with me, confuse me?"

Conner immediately looked contrite, the amusement vanishing from his expression. "I'm sorry. I was just teasing. I never know when to stop, I guess."

"Shit." Ro rubbed his forehead. "Can we get headaches? I swear I've got a mother of one building up right here."

"I dunno, I never had them when I was alive." Conner nudged his hand aside. "Let me try, okay?"

"Okay," Ro agreed. "I'm sorry. I guess we don't know each other well, really." He moaned softly as Conner used his thumbs to massage Ro's forehead, chasing away even the memory of pain there. "God, that feels good."

"I'm glad it helps," Conner murmured. "As for knowing each other, I think I know you, Ro. I've watched you for years, even though I didn't interact with you. I think some part of me knew that I'd fall toes over tits for you."

Ro huffed then snickered and peered at Conner as best he could with the man's hands on his head. "That's somehow not as romantic as head over heels, but you get points for being original."

"I'll take it. I strive to be an original." Another wink, and that delightful spark was back in Conner's expression. "But okay, you don't really know me, maybe. I'm just a man, Ro, who's been lonely for a long time. A man who lost part of himself, or hid it away, whatever. You've given me back the sexual desire I'd buried, but more than that, you make me happy, deep down inside. I'm sorry it hurts your dad and siblings, I'm sorry it hurts Sev and Laine and the people who knew you in McKinton. But I'm so fuckin' glad to have you here, in my arms."

Ro moved, putting himself in Conner's arms. Everything about Conner felt right. "Figures I'd have to die to find the perfect man." The irony of it made him want to giggle, but he held it in.

"Same goes, Ro." Conner's chest heaved with silent laughter, his breath puffing out against Ro's temple. "And before you get distracted again, let me just tell you. I went to see Laine because he'd been able to communicate with you last night, just like Sev had. I've never seen anything like that before, and I've been in this world for a long time."

Ro didn't know what to make of that, so he just murmured an encouraging sound.

"Well, I wanted to know why you could do that. I'm curious like that," Conner said, sounding proud of himself. Ro smiled and rested his head on Conner's chest as the man continued talking. "Laine was in his office, and he looked — well, he looked old and tired. It hurts seeing him and Sev grow old. I worry about what will happen when they die, you know."

"You don't want them separated in death," Ro said, realising how awful that would be for his uncles. "God, is there any way to make sure they aren't?"

He felt more than saw Conner shake his head. "Not that I know of, but maybe one of the *curanderos* or someone like that would know."

"They aren't really anyone to mess with." Ro didn't know any of the Hispanic folk healers that many called witches, but he did know they could be dangerous if they weren't good people. "Surely God or Fate or whatever there is after life wouldn't be so cruel as to keep Laine and Sev apart. That'd be hell. Literally."

"I think so too. I just have to believe they'll be together, and try my best to be there when they pass. It's gonna hurt like a mother, even if they might get to become spirits." Conner sighed. He cupped Ro's nape and thumbed the sensitive skin there. "They should always be alive, you know. I wonder if reincarnation is real."

"Maybe people go up like you said Mom did, and are sent back down as a new soul?" No, that didn't fit in his brain. "Or, not a new soul, but like a cleaned-up version, all the bad taken out and the memories dulled down before they can go into a new body. Someone said once, and it really struck me as a beautiful saying…" Ro closed his eyes, remembering. "I had a friend in high school here, and her grandpa died of cancer. She told me she hadn't said goodbye to him, because she believed that when his eyes closed in his old body, he was just blinking. He'd open them again in his new body, and I just thought that was such an amazing way to think of death."

"It really is," Conner agreed. "I think I'll adopt her theory. That makes me feel better, somehow, about those who go up. Thank you for sharing that with me." Conner brushed another of those sweet kisses over Ro's lips. "Now, I was telling you about visiting Laine this morning. He knew I was there before I even tried to tell him, and he started in about hearing you. Laine and I have this way of communicating. He'll ask me a question and I tap his shoulder or hand once for yes, twice for no, three times if he has to ask something else. It's not perfect, but it sure beats not being able to talk at all. Anyway, he said Sev thinks maybe you've always been psychic, it's just the reverse of Sev's abilities."

There went that potential headache again, trying to build up right between Ro's eyes. "So I'm only psychic when I'm dead? That's fucked up in more ways than I can count."

"Maybe, maybe not. You can communicate with the living, Sev can speak with the dead. Y'all are the flipside of each other's coin, or something like that."

Ro didn't know quite what to think of that.

Chapter Ten

Now that Conner had filled Ro in on his morning whereabouts, a distraction seemed like a damned good thing. Conner brushed away their clothes with a thought, delighting in Ro's startled gasp. He waggled his eyebrows and smirked. "What, you don't want all the other dead guys seeing us?"

"They can?" Ro asked, his face turning dark with a flush. "Really?" he squeaked.

Conner did love to tease, but Ro was looking a little too distressed for teasing to be fun so Conner let him off the hook. "Only if we want them to. I don't mind some exhibitionism, but right now I want you all to myself." And he didn't want Ro thinking about anything but him and the way they were together. "Fuck me?" he asked, hoping his blunt words would do the trick. "I stole some lube from Sev and Laine. They won't mind." They'd probably give him hell then pick on him mercilessly. Conner was looking forward to it, once everything settled down.

Ro pushed away from him, and Conner thought Ro was going to say no or scold him or something.

Instead Ro grabbed Conner's ankles and pulled. For such a little guy, Ro was strong enough. Conner yelped as he was jerked onto his back. It was a good thing he wasn't really leaning on the tree behind him or he'd have been scratched all to hell and back. Ro gave him a wicked look before pouncing on him.

"You haven't had a cock up your ass in over two decades," he said, and damn it, Conner quivered like a bowl of Jell-O in an earthquake. His mouth went dry and he couldn't squeak an answer past his lips. Ro didn't need one, apparently, because he just licked the seam of Conner's lips.

Conner parted his lips as he reached up to run his hands through Ro's glorious hair. Ro crushed his mouth to Conner's almost painfully hard. Desire burned through Conner, bringing his cock to aching fullness. He spread his legs, settling Ro's body between his thighs. Ro's slight weight felt good against his shaft, but Conner needed more. His hole clenched as he anticipated being fucked, and he let go of Ro's hair to cup his rounded ass instead.

"Soon, Con, I swear I can't wait long to be in you." Ro dropped desperate little kisses over Conner's face before delving back into his mouth. When Conner was scrambled from the kiss, Ro raised his head and stared down at him with determination and what looked like nervousness mixed together. "I've never topped, though. You'll have to tell me if I do something wrong."

Conner held back a shout of glee at being Ro's first in this way. Instead he squeezed Ro's butt, urging him on. "Just do what feels good to you. You know how to fuck."

"Well, when you put it like that…" Ro took Conner by the chin and turned his head. Conner moaned and kneaded the firm flesh in his hands while Ro sucked and licked down his neck. Conner's cock was already leaking by the time Ro pinched at his nipples, and Conner knew he wasn't going to last long at all. He tried to warn Ro, but he couldn't speak past the tightness in his chest.

Ro tweaked his nipples one last time then he slid right on down and took Conner's cock into his mouth. Conner got words out then, ones like "Fuck yeah," and "Oh my God!" The wet heat of Ro's mouth was unlike any blow job Conner could remember. He grabbed Ro's head, needing to thrust, and Ro tapped his hip. Conner took that for the okay it was and he began pumping in and out of Ro's mouth. It didn't take long with the way Ro sucked him so hard or swirled that tongue around Conner's cock. Before Conner could even work his length into Ro's throat, he was coming, groaning as his climax slammed into him and spurted out his cock.

Ro drank him down then moved lower, nuzzling Conner's sac. Conner was a melted puddle of satiation, at least for a short while. Slowly his breathing returned to normal, and he became aware of the fact that Ro was pushing on the backs of his thighs. Conner rolled his legs up, grunting from the effort of it. He still felt like he was made out of wet cotton at that point.

Then Ro tongued his ass hole, and Conner's lethargy vanished under a bolt of need. "More," he begged as he tried to spread his own cheeks apart.

Ro pushed at his hip and Conner rolled to his side. He hitched his top leg up and Ro opened him up, licking and tonguing his pucker. Conner clutched at the ground, even though he couldn't concentrate on making himself dense enough to feel it. He didn't care.

He could feel Ro sliding that slick tongue into his opening over and over again.

Conner heard the pop of the lube cap, then one slick digit was pushed into his ass. Sparks danced before his eyes. He closed them, unable not to as pleasure washed over him like a wave of tingling warmth. Ro had found his gland, gently touching it before withdrawing and pushing in again.

The second finger stretched his ring enough that it burned, but Conner pushed back eagerly, wanting to feel Ro inside him. He moaned and begged, rocked and panted as Ro fingered him. Conner's cock filled again, harder now than it'd been possibly ever. He reached down for it, needing a touch there.

"No, let me do that."

Conner peeked at Ro, saw the intense look on his face. He left off trying to jack himself and instead reached for Ro.

Ro straddled Conner's lower leg and lined his dick up to Conner's hole. As he leant down to meet Conner's one-armed embrace, he thrust, sinking in deep and hard.

Conner jolted with the penetration, damn near coming from the sudden fullness, the rub of cock over his prostate. His shout was muffled by the awkward but sweet kiss Ro gave him before sitting up and pounding away at Conner's ass.

After so many years of not being fucked, Conner craved a deep, hard claiming that would leave him feeling it. He moaned and keened as Ro slammed into him. Every time Ro's hips met his ass, Conner urged him to move harder, faster.

Ro's eyes gleamed and he growled. He took a hold of Conner's leg and held it up, opening Conner's ass more. With his other hand, Ro fisted Conner's dick, and Conner's body went into meltdown, ecstasy spiralling through him at warp speed. He barely had time to gasp before his climax hit him.

Ro cursed and drove into him again. Conner's dick spurted as Ro's shaft painted his inner walls with cum. Conner felt marked, owned, all the clichéd romantic things he'd kind of thought were just made up. Ro had him, heart and soul, that was all there was to it.

He hoped Ro never let him go. Conner hadn't really feared anything in regards to himself for a very long time, but now he feared that—and he couldn't forget seeing Alma's soul ascend into that brilliant blue sky. If he clung to Ro once the younger man pulled out and lay beside him, Conner put it down to the tender feeling of love blooming inside him. He wouldn't give any credit to the fear of being pulled up and away from his lover.

Chapter Eleven

Ro was nervous. Maybe it was silly to be nervous, considering his current state, but he was. He and Conner were waiting in Laine's office. Laine and Sev were at Ro's funeral, and Conner had offered to go with him to observe it, but Ro didn't feel right doing that. It seemed like a vain, ego-feeding sort of thing to do, as if seeing people mourn for him would ensure that he felt loved. Ro wasn't cool with that.

In the two days since his death, Ro had learnt how to pop in and out of places. Thinking of where he wanted to go, he only had to concentrate then he was there. It reminded him of his fantasies of being able to teleport when he was a kid. He just hadn't known he'd be able to do it, ever, but only if he was a spirit.

Well, it is what it is. He'd had his life, now he was lucky enough to get to have his afterlife with Conner. He just wished he hadn't hurt his loved ones by being such an idiot and swerving.

"No what-ifs," Conner told him, as if the man knew what he was thinking. Possibly he did. Ro was pretty sure there was more to Conner than even Conner knew, but he wouldn't pry.

"Trying. You can't tell me you didn't do it, too."

"For years," Conner agreed. "And it sucked. I'd rather you didn't have to go through it."

"I think we all have to. Second-guessing our mistakes when they cost us so much is human nature," he pointed out.

Conner nodded. "Sure, but you gained something too. Lucky you I'm as thick-skinned as I am thick-skulled and don't get my feelings hurt easily. I'd hate to think you were calling me a mistake."

Ro tossed a wadded-up ball of paper at Conner. "Ass. Stop trying to make me paranoid. You know what I meant."

"Yup, I did." Conner cocked his head, and his eyes glazed over. That look usually meant Sev was talking to Conner. "Sev said they'll be here in ten, and not to mess with the papers on Laine's desk."

Ro sighed, wondering if his uncle said shit like that just to get Conner to do the opposite, because that was surely what would happen.

Conner didn't disappoint him, raising every paper into the air, including the previously stuck-together sticky little yellow squares. Conner's grin was positively evil, and he looked freakin' adorable as he spun the papers around. The stapler floated up next, and in short order Laine's office walls had been redecorated. Conner was just setting the stapler back down when the office door opened. It wasn't Laine or Sev who came in, though.

Deputy Rich Montoya's eyes bugged and he turned white, bringing the scar that ran from his eyebrow to chin into stark relief. "Fuck," he mumbled, stumbling back out of the door.

"Shit!" Ro said at the same time as Conner.

Montoya's eyes didn't bug any further, they just rolled right back and he hit the floor with a thud.

"Shit! Shit, we killed him!" Ro yelled, panic flaring bright and fast. "Oh my God!"

"He's not dead," Conner said, appearing beside Rich. "I think he just passed out. If you remember, Rich had very bad experiences with spirits."

Yeah, Ro remembered. He'd been haunted, possessed even, by the spirit of the guy who'd killed Conner and had almost killed Rich. It'd taken death to get rid of the fucker, with Rich having to be revived through CPR to be free of the evil that had almost destroyed him.

"So he knows about us. Why'd he pass out?" Ro asked.

"Probably because he *heard* you," Sev said. Ro looked up to find his uncles rushing over to them. "Were you talking when he—" Sev glanced around, looking at the open office door. "He walked in the office?"

"I think all I said was 'Shit'. He startled me." Which was a lousy thing, considering Ro was the spirit.

Laine grunted and, after he and Sev had brought Rich back around, Ro was careful not to make the slightest sound. Rich had a wild look to him, like a horse frightened by thunder. Ro floated his ass back into Laine's office and started taking down the papers Conner had stapled up all over the place.

"You're not gonna let me have any fun."

Ro looked over his shoulder at Conner but didn't answer. As far as he knew, Rich was still within hearing distance. Conner started taking papers down too, grumbling as he did so. Footsteps warned Ro of someone joining them just before Laine cursed.

"Damn it to hell, Conner…"

Conner snickered and rolled up a stack of papers.

Laine narrowed his eyes. "Don't you dare—"

Conner swatted him on the backside and let the papers fall to the ground when Laine spun around.

Ro had spent his teen and early adult years being intimidated by Laine. It wasn't until he'd really matured that he hadn't been afraid of Laine snapping his head off. But even so, he couldn't have teased Laine the way Conner did.

Conner floated back and pointed. Laine's tin star pinged when it hit the ground.

"Enough!" Laine roared.

Ro opened his mouth to snap back, not caring for Laine yelling at Conner one bit.

"Don't." Conner grimaced and gestured, elevating the star until it wavered chest level with Laine. "I shouldn't have messed around today. I never do know when to quit. Or when to not even begin."

Conner sounded so disgusted with himself Ro couldn't help but hug him. "You were only teasing," he said, forgetting his attempt to keep silent with Rich nearby.

"Now isn't the time for joking," Laine snapped.

Ro glared at the man but kept silent. His balls were only so big, although what could Laine do to him now?

"He's right." Conner sighed and patted Ro's back. "I was just being an ass."

It almost hurt for him not to speak. Ro had to bite his tongue, but he didn't think Conner was an ass. Playful, happy, and deeper than anyone else suspected, that was Conner. Otherwise, he'd not have been worrying about Laine and Sev like he had.

"Rich is fine, and he won't go home," Sev said as he walked into the office. He closed the door. "He doesn't, however, want to hear a spirit speaking after his previous encounters with them, so he is manning the front desk for a while."

"I didn't mean to scare him. I thought he was you or Laine," Ro explained. "I was startled when it wasn't."

Sev looked around the office, and Ro saw it then, the age that had crept up on Sev over the years. He guessed it'd been so subtle that he hadn't realised how the years had affected Sev. On Laine, it was even less noticeable because he tended to be stern-looking, with weathered features by the time Ro had met him. But Laine's hair had once been dark, and was now almost entirely a steel-grey colour, and the lines he had were etched deeper into his skin. It saddened Ro and he shared Conner's fears for his uncles.

He realised he'd been wool-gathering while everyone else had been talking. He tuned back in, listening as Sev explained how Ro seemed to have the reverse psychic abilities of his.

"That's messed up," Ro mumbled. "Yours you could at least use while you were alive."

Sev canted his head and narrowed his eyes. "Well, but I have to wonder. How different is it being a spirit, really? Y'all get your feelings hurt, experience the same emotions and shit that we do. You feel lust—and please, don't even try to tell me you and Conner aren't going at it like bunnies. Conner broadcasts accidentally sometimes, and do you have any *idea* what it's like to be talking to a funeral director and have someone slam their orgasm into your head?"

"Oops," Conner whispered.

Sev glared daggers at him. "Oops, my ass. I walked out of there with a freakin' erection, and that was beyond disturbing."

"I'd be offended but I get what he means, even if I didn't hear exactly what he said just now," Laine said as he hooked an arm around Sev's hips. "Sev felt what Conner felt, and that wasn't something he could control."

"I didn't know." Conner didn't look overly sorry, though. "I wouldn't have invaded your privacy like that, and I wasn't trying to brag or anything. Ro just blew my mind."

"Don't say it," Sev warned.

Conner grinned. "And the rest of me, yeah, I won't name the part but—"

"Conner!"

"Fine, fine, Sev, chill." Conner dropped the subject easily and was all seriousness again. "The thing about what you can do, Ro, is that it's probably more important than what Sev can do. If other spirits find out, they'll be buzzing you to pass on messages and what have you. You won't have a moment's peace."

Ro noticed Sev gaping at Conner before he turned to explain to Laine what Conner had said. Ro frowned at them in return. Didn't they realise that Conner was pretty damned smart? Had they forgotten how he'd helped them catch killers and solve cases? Probably, he thought. Who liked to remember the bad things that happened? It was easier to focus on things like pranks and jokes.

Sev finally spoke, his voice not hiding his surprise. "Conner's right. I've had spirits hunt me down to reach the living for them, but it's really hard for most of them to clarify what they want me to do or say.

With Ro, they wouldn't have a problem, not if he can be heard as clearly as we hear him."

"What do you mean?" Ro asked.

Sev twirled a finger around, pointing at them. "We've all had some kind of brush with death, and/or spirits. Rich, too. Maybe that has something to do with why we can hear you. I don't know, though. It's just a theory, and I kind of don't believe it even if I did share it."

Conner's gleeful expression returned. "That'd be easy enough to check out. All you have to do is pop out and say 'boo' to the first stranger you see. I wish I could do that. Man, I'd have a ball!"

"So it's a good thing you can't do it," Sev told him. "Ro, why don't we go to the city park, and you can try it? I'll be close by, so that if whoever you choose to speak to hears you and freaks, we'll just say it was me."

Laine settled his Stetson lower on his brow and took Sev's hand in his. "Why not just go for a stroll and have Ro say 'hi' to people, and if they respond, Sev, you just nod like it was you who said it. Might spare someone a heart attack."

"You take all the fun out of everything," Conner muttered. "Not that I want anyone to keel over, but a yelp or two would be funny."

"Conner's bitching, ain't he?" Laine asked.

Conner slapped a hand over his heart. "He knows me too well."

"He's hamming it up," Sev told Laine. "Okay, let's do this, if you're game, Ro?"

"Why not?" Ro couldn't help but notice that Rich seemed to look right at him as they passed him by. It was unnerving, and he was sorry for freaking the guy out.

Outside, the sun was bright and hot—well, he'd bet it was hot. He didn't feel it any more than he felt the wind blowing through him. He did, however, feel Conner's hand in his as they moved along.

As soon as they reached the small park with the walking trail, Ro looked for people he didn't know. It was hard because McKinton was a small town, and he'd lived there for years. Most of the people had eaten at Virginia's Café at one time or another. That didn't mean he'd served them, but he had certainly waited on a lot of them. Still, he saw a few people he didn't think he'd ever talked to, and when he spoke to the first one, the old man answered right back. Sev's eyes went wide but he talked to the man for a few minutes before moving along.

The next two people answered Ro as well, which seemed to prove Sev's first theory that Ro could communicate with the living. He wasn't sure it was useful, but it was nice not to have lost his uncles as completely as he could have. In fact, as far as he could tell, the main difference was that hugging them was beyond his ability at that point. Conner assured him that he would learn to make himself dense for longer periods of time, but Ro wasn't so sure. Plus, by the time he learnt it, it might be too late. Or unnecessary, depending on what happened to them when they died.

Ro turned his morbid thoughts off. He wasn't going to waste the time he had with them worrying about things he couldn't control.

Back in Laine's office later, Sev seemed worried. "I just don't know what it means that you can do what you can do," he told Ro.

"Why does it have to mean anything? Maybe it's just something I can do. Maybe there's no point or reason or rhyme to it."

Conner shook his head. "I don't believe that. I think everything has a reason, and if someone like me thinks that, then it's gotta be true."

"Someone like you?" Ro cocked a brow at Conner, waiting for an explanation. If the man was dogging himself, Ro would set him straight right quick.

"Yeah, someone who doesn't have many deep thoughts. Don't have room for them when I'm always making messes of offices and such. Plus, blond hair," Conner said, confirming Ro's suspicion that he was insulting himself, even in jest.

"I'm sure there are several blonds who'd take offence to that." Ro let it go for now. He'd make sure Conner knew he was intelligent as anyone else there later when they were alone. "So what would be the point of this ability of mine?"

No one answered. Yeah, that was what Ro had thought. He supposed only time would tell if there was a purpose for him now or not. Then he looked at Conner, at his smile and dimples, and he knew that, regardless of his psychic ability, he had a purpose. Loving Conner. He'd been doing it for years, although he'd not wanted to admit it, because it had seemed pathetic to be hung up on a spirit, but it was the truth. Eventually he would share that information with Conner, but for now he was content to visit with his uncles and recline in Conner's arms.

Chapter Twelve

Conner's eyes burned as he watched Ro cry quietly. It was worse somehow than if Ro had screamed and sobbed, but Ro didn't, wouldn't, since they were in the room with Roger, Adela and Martin. A week had passed since Ro's death, and he was as surprised as Ro that Adela and Martin were still in town. Neither of them could hear the reason why, because not only were they blocked from approaching Roger, there seemed to be some sort of audible block as well. It was the oddest thing ever, and Conner had never seen or heard anything like it before—or not heard, he thought.

Either way, it extended to whoever Roger was talking with, because Adela and Martin's words were only soundless breaths to him and Ro.

"Dad," Ro tried again, but just as before, Roger didn't even bat an eyelash. Ro cupped his hands around his mouth and shouted, "Dad!"

Roger kept nodding at something Adela was saying, but—"Do it again, just like that," Conner told Ro.

This time when Ro yelled, Conner's pulse kicked up. Usually it amused him how his spirit form mimicked his former body, but right then he was over it, because he'd seen something. "Again, Ro, please."

The third time, Martin jerked his head back like he'd been slapped. He rubbed the back of his neck and unobtrusively shifted his gaze all over the room.

"He heard me?" Ro whispered, putting a hand out. It hit that invisible barrier the same as it had before. "Damn it!"

Martin stood up and said something before walking out of the room. Conner took Ro by the arm and popped them outside to where Martin was standing on the porch. The light was off and the darkness almost complete as the sky was clouded with an incoming storm.

Martin stepped up to the rail and leaned out, looking up at the clouds. "I don't know where you are, Ro, or if you can hear me, but God damn it, we miss you so bad. I was a shitty little brother, but I thought..." Martin sniffled, then sobbed, "I thought we had longer."

Ro stuffed his fist in his mouth to push back a sob of his own. Conner was going to end up crying at this rate. He caressed Ro's shoulders for a second then nudged him forward. "Try it. Just maybe like...like a little gust of air or something." If Ro spoke and Martin heard him, Martin might just go head over ass off the porch.

Ro moved closer to his brother, and Martin stopped mid-sob, hiccupping as he stood up straight and turned towards Ro. Conner watched as Ro concentrated on giving his fingers some density, then Martin's hair was brushed off his forehead and out of his eyes.

Martin opened his mouth to scream, Conner could see it coming, feel the panic like static electricity — then just as suddenly Martin slapped his hand over his mouth and stumbled backwards. He started to tip over the rail and Conner didn't think, just acted, not wanting Martin to land in the thorny rosebush below. He swooped and thought and pushed, all of which resulted in Martin shooting forward and through Ro.

Both brothers yelped, and Adela came flying out of the front door. She stopped like she'd hit that invisible wall, and she cupped her face with her hands.

"*Chingada madre*," Adela hollered, eyes wide.

"Watch your mouth, Adela," Ro snapped, probably before he could think not to.

Understandable, Conner figured, considering that his little sister had just shouted 'mother fucker' in Spanish loud enough to wake the whole neighbourhood.

Adela didn't watch her mouth, though, cuss words tumbling out as panic twisted her features. Martin ran over to her, whooshing through Ro again, which made them both gasp, but he grabbed his sister.

"Stop, before Dad comes out and sees this!" Martin said, giving her a shake. "He's already stressed to the point I'm worried he's going to have a heart attack or stroke or something!"

Conner got his arms around Ro quickly, whispering to him even though he didn't think Martin and Adela could hear him. "Give them a few minutes. They're badly rattled." Normally, Conner would have been kind of amused by their expressions, but he was learning that his sense of humour was warped and he didn't care for it much at times. "They can hear you, I think, maybe even sense you. It must just be your dad that's blocking us somehow."

"Ro?" Adela rasped shortly thereafter. "Ro, are you here? Are you—?" She glared at Martin. "I feel like a fuckin' idiot."

"Adela, your mouth," Ro said quietly. "Mama would whip your butt for that."

Adela froze, not even breathing at first as she stared at them, or at least in their direction. Martin sniffled and cupped his hands over his mouth.

Finally Adela shook herself and said, "Mama always did have a double standard for you boys and me. A lady shouldn't cuss." She rolled her eyes then promptly burst into tears.

Martin stopped covering his mouth and instead hugged his sister, but it was Ro he addressed. "How…? How can we hear you? Why are you here? Is Mama with you? Are you in Heaven or—?" He stopped and huffed. "I guess you're not in Hell, but why can't Dad hear you? I know he's angry, but that's just because that guy showed up here the morning after you died and told Dad he'd, uh, that y'all had, uh. Uh."

Conner wasn't far off from being shocked, which was hard to do to him. "That guy, the JD guy, came to talk to your dad?"

Ro squeaked and his siblings almost wet their pants, Conner would bet.

"Oh my God, oh my God, oh my God!" Martin chanted as he started backing up again. "He is here, Adela!"

"So shut up so we can hear what he has to say for himself," she scolded, crossing her arms over her chest. She tapped her foot. "Well, Ro, why were you having nasty sex with some scuzzy guy in the alley? You know he showed up here telling Dad that you two were fuck buddies and he was really going to miss the way you took his—"

"Stop!" Ro tried to double over, as if he was going to retch. Conner held onto him and rubbed between his shoulder blades, trying to comfort him. "He came here and told Dad…"

"I can't believe you're really here," Adela said, her voice full of wonder. Martin was standing, staring with his mouth gaped open. "So it's true, about the spirits? I mean, I didn't not believe Uncle Sev, but it's different. Now it is real to me. Can I touch you?"

"No," Ro said faintly. "I don't know how to do that yet. It took a lot to just move Martin's hair."

Adela looked at her younger brother and scowled. "Yeah, if he'd ditch that stupid emo haircut he might actually be cute."

"Whatever," Martin grumbled, still looking shell-shocked.

"What did Dad say?" Ro asked, sounding gutted. "God, I can't believe JD did that."

"Why not? You said he hurt you." Conner hadn't forgotten. He was going to see to it that JD paid for doing so, too. "And remember, before you answer, they can hear you, too."

"Dad said he showed up drunk, very drunk and maybe stoned from drugs, too. He looked like he'd been crying, and he told Dad it was his fault you died, because he'd been too rough when y'all had—" Adela made a lewd gesture with her hands. "Done it."

Ro scowled at her. "You can cuss like a sailor but you can't say 'when y'all had sex'?"

She wrinkled her nose as she grimaced. "Yuck. Not when it comes to my brothers. That's just disgusting. Anyway, Dad didn't say anything to anyone else, but he made JD leave and threatened to have him arrested if he came back around. He didn't want people knowing his son was being a cheap floozy in the alleyway. His words, not mine, bro."

Ro groaned and sank against Conner. "He hates me now."

"He doesn't. He hates what you did, and feels guilty that you were so lonely and lost that you did it," Adela corrected. "He thinks that if you hadn't been obligated to stay and take care of him and Mama, or at least keep them company, you wouldn't have been giving yourself away to a scumbag like JD, and you wouldn't have ended up dead." Adela took a deep breath then continued, "Dad actually begged and pleaded with Doc Hamlin not to do an autopsy. He didn't want anyone else to know about that. Doc Hamlin said he wouldn't do one, I don't know how he got around it. Maybe because the cause of death was obvious. I didn't ask. I just know that Dad is a mess, and like Martin said, maybe dangerously so."

"We can't lose him too," Martin said. "You need to stay away from him, Ro. I'm sorry, but you do."

Conner wanted to argue, but Martin wouldn't hear him, and anyways Adela was nodding and so, God damn it, was Ro.

"Yeah, yeah you're right. I already hurt everyone by being stupid." Ro tugged on his arm until Conner released him. "Look, I won't come around again. I can't get close to Dad anyway. I can't hear him, he can't hear me. I'm sorry, for all the good it does. I love y'all."

"We love you too, but it has to be this way for now." Martin stood beside Adela, who murmured her agreement. "I hope to see you when it's my time," Martin said, then Ro was flying, soaring, and Conner was right behind him, knowing Ro couldn't flee his pain. Life and death didn't work that way. He caught up to Ro in the alley of Virginia's Café. As much as Conner hated the place, he wouldn't leave Ro there to stew.

"It's done, it's the past, you can't change it," he said as Ro glared at the spot where Conner had seen him with JD.

"I don't get why Dad is so angry about it. Why he's so ashamed!" Ro threw a punch at the wall, cursing when his fist went through it effortlessly. "He's going to hate me now because I had sex with a guy here? Is that really so evil? Or is it because it was a guy? I never thought Dad didn't accept me, but maybe that was just because he hadn't had to think of me with another man."

Conner didn't think it was any of those things, or at least, it wasn't for the most part. "There are things we don't know about ourselves until something happens, some climactic event or tragedy that forces us to say or do things we wouldn't normally say or do." He moved over to Ro and stroked his hip as he spoke. "Maybe your dad was shocked, and angry, and hurt. He didn't see you as a sexual being, because he's your dad and also he never had a need to. You didn't bring guys around or even mention any. So he didn't know, and then it was right there, in his face, in the form of a drunken obnoxious fool." And that was Conner being nice in his description of JD. "He'd just lost you, and JD blabbed then your dad felt guilty, really guilty. He didn't want your name smeared in town, and maybe part of it was he didn't want it to get out for his sake, too. But really —" Conner positioned himself in front of Ro, looking into his eyes. "Really I think he did it because he wanted everyone to remember the good things about you, and even though what you did with

JD didn't negate those things, you know how people are. They love a scandal, and gossip. They'd have made it sordid—"

"More sordid," Ro corrected. "I was lonely. Mom disappeared, and you—" Ro hissed and bit his lip.

Well, that was a new guilt Conner would have to live with. He'd do it, too, because if he had contributed to Ro's need to meet JD in that alley, he'd have to find a way to make peace with that. "It's okay. I did avoid you. I wanted you and thought you pitied me, and it hurt like a mother when I saw you here with JD. I saw you before, too, with some other guy. I couldn't take it. I shouldn't have been such a coward."

Chapter Thirteen

Ro picked up right away on what Conner wasn't saying—now Conner would feel responsible for Ro's death. He'd believe that by avoiding Ro, he'd pushed him towards JD, and that in turn had led to Ro crashing.

Ro wasn't having it. He was tempted to grab Conner by his ears and rattle some sense into him, but he wouldn't. Unless it was necessary.

"Look." Ro placed his hands on Conner's shoulders and glared at him. "This is bullshit, you thinking you are in any way responsible for what happened to me. I was—am, rather—an adult. I would have put out for JD whether you popped in and said 'hi' or not, Conner. Why? Because I'm a guy, and I get horny, and all I wanted was sex, not love. Not from him, or any other guy, because I was already in love with you."

Conner opened his mouth to speak and Ro shook his head. "Let me finish. I know I said I couldn't say that, but it's true. Maybe it started out as a crush, but I heard so many stories about you, and saw how you'd interact with Sev and Laine over the years. I grew to love that man who could make them laugh and make Laine snarly and happy at the same time. I loved the way you didn't abandon them even when it seemed they only thought of you as a prankster rather than the spirit who helped them and saved them at times. I knew you before I died, Conner, and I know you now. I love you, and no one on Earth would have made me happy, because they wouldn't have been you."

"But—" Conner began and Ro decided to shut him up and make him forget whatever it was he'd been about to say. Ro climbed up Conner's body and got his legs around Conner's waist at the same time that he kissed him.

It wasn't a gentle kiss by any means, Ro clutching at Conner's muscular back, digging his heels into Conner's thighs while he nipped and bit and moaned. Conner's moan flowed into Ro, filling him with even more need. He didn't wait for Conner to will their clothes away. Ro did it himself, craving the touch and feel of his lover against him.

Conner hefted him up high, a move that wouldn't have been possible had they been living bodies, Ro didn't think. Conner braced him by the backs of his thighs and he sucked the tip of Ro's cock as Ro hung onto his head. Conner pulled him forward, taking more of Ro's length. Ro gasped and thrust, his eyes closing. The world shifted and he was on his back, Conner sucking his shaft down to the root.

Ro bucked and yelled, and Conner swallowed, his throat muscles contracting around Ro's cock with such erotic perfection that he couldn't hold back. He arched and keened as Conner pushed one thick thumb into his ass, then cum jetted from his cock. Conner drank it down. He suckled until Ro was too sensitive for another lick. Ro's dick slipped from his lips with a pop then Conner was on his knees, jerking himself off as he panted unevenly.

"Gonna come on you, Ro," he gasped, hand speeding up on his length. "Can I?"

"Please." Ro was oddly touched that Conner had asked before spraying his spunk all over Ro's belly and chest. Conner watched, wide-eyed, as each burst of cum splattered on Ro's skin. Ro ran his fingers through one splotch of it and proceeded to lick them clean as Conner moaned and licked his lips.

Ro would certainly never think of this alley the same way again. He'd avoided it, and had intended to keep doing so because he had been ashamed of what he'd done here. Now, he didn't feel guilty anymore. Maybe he'd been wrong to let JD be as rough as he had, but he refused to castigate himself over it anymore. That was in his past, and it wouldn't rule him any longer.

"Thank you," he told Conner as soon as he could speak. "I do love you."

Conner scooped him up, rubbing against Ro's sticky chest. "I love you too, Ro. I have for a long time. I don't even remember when, exactly, because it's been in here so long." Conner leant back and started to reach between them. "Eh." The spunk vanished and Conner grinned. "So much easier to clean up than when I had to actually breathe to survive."

Ro laughed, delighted to have the man he'd dreamed of for so long in his arms.

* * * *

They checked in on Sev and Laine, and, though Ro hated to, he told them about the confrontation with Adela and Martin. Laine was not happy about Roger begging off the autopsy, but he said they weren't necessarily required. Ro didn't know if they were or not, but he was actually glad his family had been spared the details.

"Still, I want a chat with this JD fella," Laine growled, glaring at the door like he was just about to head out to find JD.

"Why?" Ro asked. "He didn't do anything I didn't let him."

Laine glared in his direction then. "Yeah, and I'd tell you to stop fucking strangers in alleys but now you and Conner are—" He made a wavering gesture with his hand.

Ro wished Laine could see him roll his eyes. "Oh my God, seriously? Why is it you and Adela can't say 'you and Conner are having sex'?" Ro leaned over until his lips would have been touching Laine's ear if he'd had an actual body. "He loves me, and I love him."

"Jesus!" Laine hollered, swatting at Ro. "Don't *do* that! I swear Conner's a bad influence."

Sev was laughing so hard he was wheezing, and he soon had tears streaming down his cheeks. Ro obviously wasn't going to get anything sensible out of him.

"Did you even hear what I said?" he snapped at Laine.

"Yeah, yeah, y'all love each other," Laine said nonchalantly.

Ro was getting pissed off then, but Laine finally smiled, and not the little one he usually gave, but a big, happy one. "That's great, guys. I'm happy for you both. Makes me feel better about what'll happen after we pass away, too."

Sev stopped laughing then and swiped at his cheeks. Laine stood up and gathered Sev in his arms. "No matter who goes first, or if we die together, we won't ever leave each other."

"No, we won't," Sev agreed, and Ro hoped and prayed that they were right. Conner looked away from them and put a hand on his chest.

Ro had seen him do that before, become contemplative and push at his chest, as if feeling for something or holding something back. He popped them both out of the house and back into the meadow where they'd first made love. There in the sunlight, he saw fear etched in Conner's features.

"What's wrong?" he asked, icy tendrils of dread tracing his insides.

Conner looked up again, squinting at the clear blue sky. "Before you died, I was just thinking about things. I saw your mama's soul when she passed. She went right up into that great big blue. She was so bright, Ro. Crystal clear, pure, and she moved so fast. She was just gone, and that terrified me. Something tugged at me here, maybe because I'd been restless, questioning things, I don't know. But it felt like an invisible cord was pulled, and it was tied to my soul and strung up all the way to the ends of the sky. It was like a suctioning in my chest, and I didn't want to go. I don't want to leave this existence." He looked down at Ro. "I don't want to leave you."

"I won't let you," Ro promised, "not without me, not ever. If you go, I go, and that's all there is to it. Whatever happens next after this afterlife, it will happen to us both."

Conner glanced at the sky again then sighed and hugged Ro, resting his chin on the top of Ro's head. "I'm holding you to that promise."

"You do that, Conner. I'll keep it." He wouldn't let anything separate them. Death had brought them together, and not even a new life would tear them apart.

"Now come on, let's go see what we can hide from Sev to give him something to yell at us about. I'm pretty sure he and Laine are busy bumping uglies." Ro waggled his eyebrows at Conner. "No popping in. First one there gets a blow job!"

"Like that makes either of us a loser?" Conner laughed, and the race was on.

Chapter Fourteen

Conner heard the scream even though he and Ro were miles away. Ro heard it too, his eyes just huge in his head as Adela's panicked voice rent the air.

"Dad," Ro said at the same time it clicked in Conner's head. Adela hadn't left McKinton when Martin did. She'd stayed to take care of Roger.

"Come on." Conner knew Ro was in a stupor, held in place by absolute terror. He took Ro's hand and had them at Roger's before a second had passed. The usual barrier that had held them back was gone, and they arrived to find Adela with the cellphone on the floor beside her dad as she performed CPR on him.

"Don't, oh, Ro, help me, help him!" she pleaded, sweating as she gave Roger chest compressions.

"What do I do?" Ro asked, tears filling his eyes. At that moment, Conner saw it, the bright circular pulsing of Roger's soul as it began to pull free of his body. It wasn't the same brilliant glowing form Alma's was, perhaps tinted grey by Roger's guilt and anger. "No," Ro howled, which made Adela scream and pound on Roger's chest. Over the phone the emergency service dispatcher squawked out directions no one was paying attention to.

"Tell Adela to get her shit together and keep doing the CPR right," Conner said, hoping he sounded like someone to be obeyed. He wasn't the bossy type, but he needed them to listen.

"Don't stop, Adela, keep working on him," Ro got out between sobs. Conner watched Roger's soul hover, half in and half out of his body. "In, in, in," Ro muttered, obviously seeing it too. "Get back in there, Dad, please. I know you miss Mom, but Adela and Martin need you, too. Mom would want you to stay and take care of them."

"Like I took care of you?" Conner heard, a faint whisper on the wind as the front door flew open.

"It wasn't your fault," Ro said. Conner held up a finger, pointing to the EMS workers running their way. Ro bit his lip and Roger made his departure then, his soul shooting up.

Conner was moving before he could talk himself out of it. He felt it, that tug reeling him up and up like a trout on a hook. It terrified him more than anything had, because he knew, he *knew* that if he went too far, he'd never be able to come back to Ro.

Roger's soul wobbled and wasn't as fast as Alma's, but it was still zooming right on up. Conner forced himself to keep going, up and up until he was past the trees and could only faintly hear Ro's shouts, calling his name.

God help me. He can't lose both of us. But Conner couldn't turn back, not when he could almost touch that grey-bright blob. "Roger, damn it! Don't make Ro lose us both! Don't be a coward and give up now!"

Conner went up farther still, until there was nothing but that bright blue sky around him and Roger. He felt his form waver, as if he were changing. *No, no, no, no! Not now, not now, please, God, if You're there, please don't take me now!*

He began to fold in on himself, or perhaps he was turning inside out, Conner didn't know. He screamed in fury and fear and lunged up, his fingers brushing Roger's soul. The touch was like a shock, hurting him, but Conner didn't stop. "You can't have me yet!" he bellowed to whoever would listen. "And Roger, stop being a selfish ass!"

Whether it was luck or Roger finally listening to him, Conner didn't know, but suddenly he and Roger both were plummeting down at a startling speed. Even already dead, Conner was scared shitless. He screamed the entire way down, Roger's soul making an odd whistling noise as it accompanied him.

Conner fully expected pain when he hit the ground, but instead he stopped suddenly, lying right beside Roger's body. He heard Ro's yell but was amazed by the sight of Roger's soul slamming back into him. Roger's body went from a grey, lifeless thing to a living, breathing—well, coughing and gasping—man again.

Ro tackled Conner and they were gone, back into their meadow.

"Don't you ever scare me like that again!" Ro screamed at him. "I can't lose you, Conner. Not you!"

Conner felt like his insides had been taken apart, tossed in a blender, and turned on purée before being poured back into him. And he didn't even have insides, as far as he knew!

"Dad… Losing him would be horrible, but he's older, and he wants to be with Mom," Ro was babbling, waving one arm all over while clutching Conner with his other hand. "But you, Jesus Christ,

Con, that would kill me all over again. I tried to follow you, but you were just gone and I couldn't catch up no matter how fast I went. I saw it, you started to glow." Ro's eyes were huge, his complexion pale as he talked. "It started at your chest, then you kind of, it was like you started to shrink, and turn the same colour as the sky. I'll hate that colour forever, and longer than that! What was that, Conner?"

Conner rubbed his chest, fearful he'd feel that tug again, but he didn't. He looked into Ro's eyes and felt a peace different from any he'd had before. He didn't know what that place was, but he wasn't afraid of it, not anymore.

"I think it's the next level, what comes after this, when we're ready for it." Conner looked up into the bright sky for the first time in a while without the dark edges of fear peeking at him. "I think that maybe we can stay here if we're needed, or we can go on up there and get another chance. Maybe watch over our loved ones in a different way, as a new soul on Earth. I don't know for sure, but this is true." He turned his focus back to Ro, loving everything about the man. "I won't go without you, and I won't ever have to. Whatever happens next happens for us together. If that means we're born again and start life all over, I'll find you, and I'll love you until we die then, and it'll be that way, always."

And it would be, Conner swore, as he took Ro into his arms. There were some truths that were indisputable, and the fact that he and Ro belonged together was one of them.

"Me too, I swear," Ro said against his lips. Conner didn't doubt it. He kissed Ro there, under that sky he'd nearly lost himself in, and he knew their souls would always find each other. Neither death nor life would keep them apart.

WHIRLWIND

Dedication

J.G., L.N., I'm holding y'all to those cookies and
margaritas in Atlanta :)

It's easy to remember all the bad things we've done,
all the mistakes we've made,
the imperfections we have.
Remembering to love ourselves, to forgive and try
again, is much harder,
but so very worth it.

Chapter One

Stefan Bausch nudged his friend Ro. "Wanna play football?"

Ro looked horrified for a moment, his eyebrows scrunching together as he gawked at Stefan. "Why would I want to do that? I hated football when I was alive, and what would we use for a ball?"

"A ball," Stefan said blandly. "Don't tell me you haven't learnt how to pick things up yet. You're with Conner. You'd have to know how to grab corporeal things just to keep up with him."

Ro scowled. "That still doesn't answer the why part."

"Because," Stefan said as he waggled his eyebrows, "think of the way everyone at the park would freak out if they saw a ball shooting back and forth through the air." It'd be hilarious…maybe. *Or maybe not, since a lot of the townsfolk believe in spirits—ghosts.* Stefan wasn't interested in being exorcised. Again.

"Sounds like a great way to freak out someone and end up cast out of this world and into whatever comes next," Ro muttered, crossing his arms over his chest. "Didn't something like that happen before?"

How did Ro know what he'd been thinking? Stefan rolled his eyes. "Yeah, yeah, and it sucked. It was your grandparents who did it, wasn't it?"

"I don't want to talk about them." Ro glanced around. "You know I still fear that they're gonna pop up just to try to ruin my afterlife."

"Conner would handle them," Stefan informed his friend. Ro had to know that. Conner would never let anyone hurt Ro.

Ro flipped his long black hair. "Sure he would, but I don't want him to have to. Anyway, I'm pretty sure they would hang around the other part of the family, not the heathen gay side."

"Maybe." But sometimes Stefan got so bored he wished someone jerkish would show up. All the spirits he knew were nice—and either straight or hooked up, like Conner and Ro.

"We could go see what's happening at Sev and Laine's place," Ro offered, a hopeful light springing up in his eyes. "Conner's off greeting newcomers." Ro's joy died down and his expression shifted into one of sadness. "How he knows when someone's going to pop up is beyond me. And him, too, actually. He says he just feels this tug in his chest." Ro shook his head. "That sounds creepier than us being dead in the first place. Oh man, I sure hope whoever does show up isn't a psycho criminal. I always worry, but I don't know why. It's not like a psycho spirit could kill us all over again. I need to quit watching the news. It's all bad shit. Why can't everyone just get along?"

"That's asking a lot of humanity," Stefan scoffed. He thought about going with Ro and shook his head.

"You go on. I'm in a weird mood and should probably just go off and pout for a while."

"Are you sure?" Ro uncrossed his arms and reached for Stefan's hand. Ro's skin was warm and soft, his grip firm and comforting. "I'd love to have your company."

Seeing Laine and Sev wasn't a bad thing, but Stefan didn't want to hang around another happy, loving couple. Laine and Sev were definitely that. They'd been together forever and still acted like they'd only just met and fallen in love. It was sweet, and caused an ugly spike of jealousy to rear up in Stefan. He hated that about himself.

"Nah, really, I need to just chill out." Sleep, maybe. Stefan could sleep in his ghostly form just like he had in his live-bodied form. It helped to pass the time when he was bored stiff.

"You sure?" Ro asked again.

Stefan barely refrained from rolling his eyes again. "I'm sure. Jeez, go before I start thinking you're afraid I'll float off to the Great Beyond or whatever."

"Don't even joke about that," Ro snapped. "It's not funny."

"Sorry," Stefan said immediately. Ro had almost lost Conner to the Great Beyond or whatever came after when Conner had gone chasing after a spirit. It'd been a close call. None of them knew what happened to them once they went up, up and away. None of them wanted to find out, either.

"Really, I'm sorry. I told you I need to go pout. I'm not fit company." Stefan pulled Ro in for a hug. "I'm an asshole."

"Love you anyway," Ro huffed, but the tone of his voice as he said it took the sting out of him not disagreeing with Stefan's self-description.

"You too." Stefan patted Ro's back then stepped out of the embrace. "Go watch the lovebirds. I'm gonna head to the cemetery."

Ro shivered. "That's so morbid."

"I don't think it is. I like seeing the headstones with the long lives carved onto them. Makes me happy those people had a long time with their loved ones." Stefan nodded. "Catch ya later!"

Stefan let himself float up a few feet then he shot up high and fast before angling towards the graveyard. He hadn't been lying to Ro. He *was* glad for the folks who didn't die young like he had—it gave him hope for his brother and Darren, as well as other people he cared about who were still living. Stefan didn't want them to die, but if they did, or when they did, rather, he hoped they'd stay here on Earth with him.

As for being alive, he didn't miss it. It probably made him a weirdo to like being dead a heck of a lot more than he'd liked being alive, but since he *was* dead, Stefan figured it was okay. Surely being a spirit in the afterlife entitled him to some quirks.

Well, more quirks. Stefan didn't like to think back on his life much. He'd been deemed 'developmentally slow' and jeez, it'd been hard. People had picked on him, bullied him. Johnny Chapman had even killed Stefan over it.

Stefan shuddered. Johnny had done it in the worst way possible for Stefan. First he'd led Stefan on, made him think Johnny actually cared about him. Stefan had been so lonely, and so eager to please everybody, but especially Johnny since he used to pay attention to Stefan.

Never around other people, though. Johnny had explained how being seen with Stefan would kill his cool cred. That had hurt, but Stefan got it. His brain was damaged, and that always made people steer clear of him no matter how happy and giggly he'd been.

And so he'd let Johnny touch him, hurt him in other ways that he'd thought were supposed to be enjoyable. They hadn't been, but Stefan had been desperate for companionship. Darren had been Stefan's only friend, and even so, Stefan had known Darren was slipping away from him. Stefan might have been slow, but he wasn't totally stupid.

Except for believing Johnny. That had got Stefan pushed over a cliff, literally. Stefan's greatest fear, besides being abandoned by everyone he loved, was of heights.

No, not of heights. Of falling from somewhere high up. Or being pushed. Johnny's laughter had been pure evil as he'd shoved Stefan over that cliff. Stefan had had one single second, less than, even, where he'd felt like he was floating. Then he'd been filled with a terror so great it had crushed him. He hadn't even been able to scream as tears had sprouted from his eyes.

The moment of impact had been the worst. Pain had slammed through every nerve ending in his body, shooting up from the hard ground and rocks he'd landed on. He'd had no idea anything could hurt so bad.

But the pain had ended quickly, and Stefan had found himself drifting, looking down at the gross mess of his body. Dead or not, that image still gave Stefan nightmares.

Stefan shuddered again. Being a spirit was so much better than being alive. He could feel himself—his body was as real in form to him now as it had been before he'd died. Just like he could shudder and all the other stuff he used to do, basically. Breathing was optional, but it just felt too creepy to not do it.

What Stefan had come to realise in the years since he'd passed away was that his physical body truly was gone. His spirit had remained behind, and the whys and hows of that were beyond him, but his corporeal limitations no longer existed.

In other words, it'd been his brain that had been damaged, not his spirit. Granted, he'd been slow to catch on, but after a lifetime of not being as bright as he'd always longed to be, he hadn't known to expect any different. Stefan wasn't even going to think about how many years he'd wasted being dead and still not realising he was free of those physical restrictions. He'd figured it out one day when his brother Lee had been trying to do his taxes. Stefan had been able to add up all the figures in his head accurately, and quicker than Lee could with a calculator.

It had been odd to suddenly realise he wasn't slow like he used to be. Although, considering it'd taken him years to do so, maybe he wasn't the brightest star in the sky.

So overall, he preferred being dead. He wasn't as lonely as he'd been when he'd been living. There were times, yeah, when he was miserable, when he wondered what the point of everything was. Then he'd get distracted from his moodiness and be happy again.

His astral body was better than his physical one had ever been too. Not necessarily bigger or anything, but it worked like it should have. When he'd been alive, half the time it had seemed like his brain hadn't quite managed to tell his arms and legs how to move right. He'd trip and fall, and people would laugh—but that wasn't a problem anymore.

No, now he was free of the physical chains of the mortal realm. Stefan snorted. He was still a goofball, and he was bored. *Maybe I'll go spy on Conner and the new guy. Or people.* With the latest oil boom in Texas the population had nearly doubled. There were buildings thrown up in a rush—hotels, motels, restaurants and bars. Oil workers and rig drivers were all over, too. It was getting crowded.

Even for the dead. The influx of people meant more fatalities on the roads. Stefan didn't like to think about how many wrecks he'd seen in the past year and a half. Yet no one seemed to learn. People still sped like their ass was on fire, and drinking and driving must have been a competitive sport for some. Drug use was on the rise, too, so yeah, more dead people. A few of them hung around once their bodies had keeled over.

Stefan had friends in his spiritual world, and he had his family in the living one. All in all, he was happy.

He was just… Bored. As. Hell.

Oh well. He'd go to the graveyard, see if he could work out his weird mood, then if he needed a little excitement, he'd go poke Lee in the armpit or something.

Chapter Two

Dead. I'm dead. Gideon Crosby stared down at his body, or what was left of it. Other soldiers were hurt, but him? *Dead.* Then he saw Jordan Dempsey lying there, gasping, blood bubbling from his lips. *No! God, no, please –*

How it was possible for him to be dead and still hurt like his heart was literally being ripped from his body was a mystery that Gideon didn't care to unravel. All that mattered in that moment was that his best friend was dying, too.

Which meant Gideon had failed. "I'm so sorry, Jordan. God damn it, I'm so sorry." Gideon sobbed, but no one seemed to hear him. There were soldiers shouting orders, soldiers screaming in pain. Even if he'd been alive, would anyone have noticed him, would they have heard the agony in his voice as he watched Jordan's blue eyes widen with shock?

His own death was nothing. Gideon had already pushed the trauma of it aside as he floated – *levitated? What the hell am I doing?* – towards Jordan. He wasn't sure how he did it, but he needed to be with Jordan, then he just…was. Gideon reached for Jordan automatically, the need to stem the blood flowing from his chest irresistible.

But Gideon's hands went right through Jordan. Gideon gasped, jerking his hands back, sure he'd feel something. Gideon stared at his hands until Jordan made another wet, sickening sound. He looked at Jordan, and to his surprise, found those blue, teary eyes focused on him.

"Jordan?" Gideon rasped, reaching again for his friend, the only one he'd ever had, really.

"Gid… Hurts," Jordan got out in what was barely even a whisper. Gideon cringed. At least he'd died quickly. There'd been massive pain, thunderous noise ripping through his head, then nothing but confusion as he'd risen above his remains. But Jordan was suffering.

"Let go," Gideon urged. "Jordan, let go. Don't fight it. There's no way—" He swallowed around a tight knot of regret. He'd say it, if it put an end to Jordan's suffering. "There's no way they can save you." Not with the amount of blood Jordan had lost, or the wounds he had suffered. Gideon averted his gaze, staring only into Jordan's eyes. "Let go, and it won't hurt. It'll just—"

Even staring at Jordan, Gideon caught a flash of brilliant white-gold light shooting up from a nearby soldier's body. He had to follow that light visually. Where was it going?

Up, up and away. Since I'm not going up—and I'm not going down, thank God—what does that mean?

Jordan gasped, or tried to. Gideon jerked his attention back to his friend. "It'll be okay, Jordan. We'll figure this out together." If Jordan didn't go shooting up into the heavens. Gideon was terrified he would and that would mean Gideon would be all alone in the world, or spiritual plane, whatever it was he was existing on. But he didn't want to be a selfish bastard, either. If what was up beyond the clouds was better, then he wanted Jordan to go there.

Jordan blinked, and when his eyes opened again, his body gave up the fight. His spirit rose up, jetting high into the air.

"No!" Jordan screamed. He clawed at nothing, and Gideon willed himself to help his friend. He willed it, then he was up there too, wrapping his arms around Jordan's legs and *feeling* him.

They began sinking, slowly at first, then it was a sudden, rapid plummet to the ground. "Shit!" Gideon got out right before twisting around so he'd bear the brunt of the fall.

Except they didn't hit. They just kind of...stopped. Gideon opened his eyes, not even knowing when he'd closed them. "Oh God," he groaned when he saw that they were almost completely *in* the ground. It was too close to being buried for him. "Get up! Get up, get up, get up!"

He'd always been claustrophobic. Apparently being dead wasn't going to change that. It wasn't until he was panting and shoving his way to his feet that he realised he probably could have just floated right up through Jordan. Jordan had felt pretty solid, that was the problem.

"Jesus Christ, look at us," Jordan whispered.

Gideon looked at Jordan, thinking the man speaking of them as they were at that very moment. Jordan wasn't. He was staring aghast at their bodies.

"Stop looking at it," Gideon said as he hooked an arm around Jordan's neck. "It won't do any good, and we aren't in there anyway."

"This is going to kill my mom," Jordan muttered before sobbing. He fisted a hand and pushed it against his mouth.

"You don't have to be quiet. No one else can hear us." Gideon opened his arms up and Jordan hesitated a moment. "We're dead, Jo. I don't really think there's any need to worry about pride and machismo at this point."

They'd never so much as hugged before. A slap on the back, nudge of shoulders or fist bumps, yeah, they'd done those. Hugging was weird for them both, or at least, Gideon thought it was as weird for Jordan as it was for him.

"Your mom's a strong person," Gideon murmured, hoping he was saying the right things. "She'll get past this. She won't get over you" — Jordan sobbed. *Shit, shit, shit! Wrong thing to say!* — "but she'll get past it, Jo. She will. Maybe someday she'll, er…maybe we can go check on her."

Gideon figured he deserved props for catching himself before he told Jo maybe someday his mom would join them as ghosts. He frowned. Ghosts sounded so cheesy, like something that didn't exist except as a TV show gimmick. He guessed it didn't really matter at that point.

"We could go back to that little Texas town you're always talking about hating so much," Gideon rambled on. "Go see it, keep an eye on your mom."

"What's gonna happen to us?" Jordan asked in a rough voice. "I never believed in ghosts. How can we be something that doesn't exist? What if…" He pushed out of Gideon's hold. Excitement lit up his entire expression. "What if we aren't dead? Or you aren't, or I'm not? Something, I mean. What if one or both of us is in a coma somewhere and this is a totally fucked-up dream?"

Gideon almost wished it was. Well, he definitely wished they were both still alive, but being in a coma was almost as scary as being dead. He shook his head. "Jo, I didn't dream that blast, or the pain."

Jordan's face crumpled for a split second then he straightened his back and tipped his chin up. "So fine. We're dead, then. Now what? We just hang around here and haunt people? Oh." The sneaky, troublemaking look that Gideon knew so well settled over Jordan's features. "Oh yeah, I'm gonna haunt the fuck out of the assholes who did this!"

Gideon swung around and gestured at the point of impact on the ground, a large, scorched area. "Think he's toast, bud."

"Damn it!" Jordan glanced around furtively. "He's not here, is he?"

"Nope. Just us. I saw some people go up," he pointed at the sky. "Don't know where that guy went."

Jordan grunted and rubbed his eyes. They were red-rimmed, and his cheeks were wet with tears.

"You really did cry." Gideon held up a hand when Jordan opened his mouth to speak. "Don't tell me I'm an idiot for stating the obvious, and it wasn't a jab at your manhood. It's just that I'm surprised. I don't know what we are, what we can do. Other than touch each other, and sink into the ground." Gideon remembered something else. "One other thing. When I wanted to get to you, I thought really hard about it, then *poof*, there I was at your side."

"Poof?" Jordan asked, raising his right eyebrow in a familiar look of disdain. "Did you really just say poof?"

Gideon was going to be the better man and not point out that Jordan had just bawled like a baby all over him. Besides, he knew Jordan was mostly teasing. If he was being any kind of mean at all, it was because he *had* broken down and cried.

Despite the 'sensitive male' crap Gideon had heard women wanted, every guy he knew thought crying equalled weakness. Gideon didn't, and he didn't care what women thought of him for the most part, not if they were looking to hook up with him. Lady bits did nothing for him and never had. Jordan raised his left eyebrow as well and Gideon took a second to remember whatever it was Jordan had asked.

"Yeah, I said poof. Get over it." Gideon shook his head. "We're going to argue about shit like the word poof? We're dead, Jordan." He'd never pussy-footed around anyone or any subject since he'd become an adult.

"I know." Jordan ran a hand through his hair and looked past Gideon. "God."

"Stop looking," Gideon said with only a hint of exasperation.

"Can't. I see Morty's body. Fuck. His wife just had that baby…" Jordan trailed off as he pinched the bridge of his nose. "I don't know what to do, Gid. I don't know how to live—exist—like this. Why didn't I go up? Is there no heaven? No hell?"

Gideon couldn't help but to glance up at the sky. At least he wasn't boiling hot anymore under the sun's rays. "I don't know. I've never been religious anyway, so you're really asking the wrong person."

Jordan let loose a laugh that sounded more like he was choking. His lips were curled up in a smile, which was how Gideon knew he wasn't choking. That, and he didn't think it was possible to choke now.

"Let's go home, Gid." Jordan sighed heavily and took one last look at their surroundings. Sadness seemed to leak out of his pores. "I don't even know where that is now, but I'm hoping maybe it's McKinton, Texas."

Chapter Three

One of the oil field workers, a short, stocky man who smelt like he'd worked hard all day, had caught Stefan's eye. Stefan didn't mind the man-sweat odour. It wasn't like he was going to have sex with the guy or anything. He just appreciated the way the man moved. Sensuously, like a human-cat hybrid or something. He moved like sex, that was it!

Stefan saw the name on the man's credit card when he took it from his wallet to slide it into the gas pump's card reader. *Wallace W. Whitaker. Boy, someone's mommy and daddy had a thing for alliteration.* That was okay—Stefan just enjoyed the way the guy held himself, the way he walked. There was confidence in them he was going to try his damnedest to mimic.

Stefan puffed up his chest. Wow, that made his lower back kind of ache. He eyed Wally again. Okay, so Wally just had a bulkier chest. Stefan glanced down at his own torso. He was kinda scrawny, but not a total twig. He pulled his shirt out from the collar so he could peer down it. He was close to having some little moobs going on in there. Not that he actually *had* man boobs. His pecs just weren't rock-hard, and sometimes his nipples got hard and pointy, even puffy if he played with them enough.

Still, his chest was soft, he guessed. All of him was. He was lean, but he didn't have a six-pack, or even a four-pack. Hell, he didn't even have a bottle or a can on his abs. There was nothing but pale, smooth, hairless skin and honestly, Stefan liked the way it felt under his hands.

He'd *really* like to feel a hard, muscular body under his hands, but that wasn't likely. His one foray into checking out a gay club—with the reasoning that maybe other gay spirits would be horny and hanging around—had been a bust.

Besides, with everyone he knew in happy monogamous relationships, he couldn't have gone through with fucking around. Probably. It would have made him feel cheap.

Or really happy.

Stefan slapped his own cheek lightly. "Head out of the gutter, man."

Of course, Wally had to reach down and rub his cock through his hideous orange work jumpsuit right then. Stefan moaned as his own shaft grew erect. Wally kept rubbing himself as he eyed a big-busted redhead shaking her ass as she walked into the gas station. The sight did nothing for Stefan, but Wally sure liked it.

He liked it enough to get in his truck and immediately whip out his pecker. Stefan grimaced. *Well,* that *was a disappointment.* Stefan tried not to be a penis snob when he was indulging his voyeuristic tendencies, but Jesus, that was just pathetic.

"So much for that bravado." He gave Wally's extra thumb a scathing glance then left to find Lee. Maybe he'd be doing something interesting. Hopefully not having sex with Darren. Stefan would cop to having peeked on them some when they'd first started messing around. He hadn't spied on them all the way. That would have been too many kinds of wrong, and while he'd seen his brother Lee naked before, it'd been in a totally different context. Watching Lee fuck anyone would have almost been incestuous.

Watching Darren, however, had been an eye-opener. Just like watching Laine and Sev—talk about sex ed! The things those two did… Stefan shivered and palmed his cock through his jeans. Going to the room Lee and Darren had set aside just for him sounded like a better idea than seeking out Lee. Stefan had the urge to beat off until he passed out from coming so much.

In the blink of an eye, he was in his room. Despite not being able to see him, and despite the fact that Stefan didn't need any of it, his brother and Darren had fully furnished the bedroom. There was a queen-sized bed and a dresser along with a nightstand that all matched. Darren had also put a laptop in the room. Every now and then, Stefan could focus enough to tap out a short message. It took a lot of energy, though, so he didn't do it often.

Conner could write a whole goddamned novel on that thing. Stefan huffed in annoyance as he made his clothes disappear. He wanted to be as strong as Conner was someday, but it wasn't going to happen. Conner's spirit had been a dynamic one when he'd been alive. Stefan's, not so much.

Stefan did tap a few buttons to get the porn playing. That was worth expending some energy for. It didn't take him long to get off as he watched the action on the screen. Two rough, gruff bear-types battled it out for dominance before the one with less grey in his hair pinned the older-looking one down and fucked him. That was hot, but the kiss they shared as the younger guy slowly pushed into his man was way sexier than the actual sex was.

Stefan didn't last past the kiss, but he never did. There was a tenderness in those men's expressions that couldn't be faked. If they *were* faking it, they needed to get to acting in Hollywood movies pronto. They'd take every acting award there was.

Coming felt just as good as it had when he'd been living. Stefan moaned and clenched his butt as his orgasm spiralled up from his balls to spurt out of his slit. His cum was still warm and sticky on his skin, the scent still pungent and tangy. Stefan barely managed to keep his eyes open so he could see that kiss.

God, he wanted to be kissed like that. Getting fucked would be good, too. He thought he'd like it way better than he had before. He was older now, more mature in so many ways, and he'd spied on enough men getting fucked that he knew it wasn't usually the painful thing he'd experienced under Johnny's demanding body.

Stefan shook his hand, sending spunk splattering, except it didn't stay where it landed. Almost as soon as it hit, it evaporated. Stefan snorted as one splotch of it began disappearing off the dresser mirror. The stuff would stay on *him* until he willed it gone. Why did it vanish on other objects? Maybe because it didn't exist outside of him.

He'd long ago given up trying to make sense or rules for what being a spirit meant. There were some basic rules, sure, like concentrating to firm up and let a living body feel you. How to move from place to place, how to think up clothes if you wanted them—most everyone did. Stefan had only encountered a couple of nude spirits, and like the tales he'd heard about nude beach enthusiasts, he had to think it'd have been better for those particular spirits to remain clothed.

Okay, he could be a snobby little shit at times. Stefan knew he wasn't perfect even if his spiritual brain was better than his physical one had been. He had the tendency to be a brat when he didn't get his way, and he still liked peeking in on people when he shouldn't, but jeez, that was about the only kind of sex he had unless he was beating off.

That didn't justify him being a voyeur and he knew it. Stefan swore he'd stop. In all fairness, he hadn't expected that Wally guy to pull it out and start whacking off at the gas station earlier. If he'd had any idea how disappointed he'd be upon seeing Wally's bits, he'd surely have split a lot sooner.

Stefan looked down at his own cock. It was about average length, he guessed, six inches or so, but it was thick and veiny, and kind of on the ugly side because of it. He'd seen pretty dicks—long, elegant, pink, brown, mahogany, tan, ivory almost even, with sweet curves to them, or straight as a rail. The ones with only a thin vein or two were the ones he thought were gorgeous. His looked kinda too veiny in his opinion, but it didn't really matter. It wasn't like he was waving it around at anyone.

Stefan tipped his head and listened. He grinned and thought his clothes back on as he was shooting through the air. Walls, schmalls, he went through them too until he was back outside and able to flutter Lee's hair with ghostly fingers.

"Ack!" Lee spun around and swatted at him, much to Stefan's delight. "I hate that! It gives me the heebie-jeebies, like someone's dancing on my grave or something."

Stefan had never really understood that phrase. How would being creeped out make someone feel that they were psychic and aware of something that would happen after their death? It was just a stupid saying. He needed to quit over-analysing it.

"Can you get the water?" Darren asked as he got out of the car with recyclable canvas grocery bags hanging from his arms. "I've got the food."

"Yeah." Lee opened the back passenger door. "Too bad Stef can't help us carry everything in."

It wasn't like Stefan was going to be using any of the groceries, but he wouldn't have minded helping. Times like that, he did miss being alive after all. Conner could cause a whirlwind that would lift up the groceries. Stefan wasn't that talented — yet. But he was determined to get there some day. Conner said he was strong, and stubborn, a combination that should do him good except for when he put his mind to doing something he ought not to.

Stefan settled for whipping up a brisk wind around the chickens. Darren hated one of them in particular, a Rhode Island Red that was hell-bent for Darren's blood. The original bird that had been here years ago had long since passed on, and though Darren had sworn he hated that rooster, he'd gone right out and bought another one. There'd always been a mean, aggressive rooster on the property ever since.

"Stefan!" Darren yelped as the rooster squawked and came at him. Stefan giggled and managed a gust of wind that put Sweety, the inappropriately named red rooster, slightly off course. Good thing too, since

Darren was wearing shorts. His legs would have been left bloody by ol' Sweety.

The rooster shook out his feathers and flapped his wings. Stefan had a hard time not being intimidated by the evil look in the bird's beady eyes. The rooster clucked and cocked his head. Stefan wondered if the rooster could see him or sense him somehow. It wasn't the first time an animal had seemed to be aware of him.

Sweety let out a warning squawk right before launching himself at Stefan. Stefan didn't think it was a lucky guess on the bird's part, either. Stefan shot up a good six feet in the air and barely kept from yelping. The rooster couldn't hurt him.

It was a moot point, just like having his heart slam against his ribs in rapid staccato was. He didn't *have* an actual heart, and couldn't fathom why his mind insisted on reliving sensations he hadn't particularly enjoyed the first time around—who the hell enjoyed panic and borderline terror?

"I'm going to choose to believe Stefan just sacrificed himself for my safety," Darren said as he hurried up the porch steps. "Why is it I keep replacing those mean roosters when they die?"

"Because you're a masochist?" Lee suggested, which earned him a light kick to his backside when he joined Darren on the porch. "Careful, wouldn't want you to damage the goods." Lee waggled his eyebrows and shook his butt.

Stefan made gagging noises even though he knew they wouldn't hear him. God, he really was surrounded by happy couples. *And evil chickens.*

That was it. He was going to go brood in the graveyard. Stefan fluttered around his brother for a second. He wanted a hug so bad, but—in a heartbeat he was soaring, outside, the sky blue and bright surrounding him.

The town of McKinton was laid out in almost a perfect square now. Before the oil boom, only Main Street had been very built up. Now there were buildings all over.

The graveyard wasn't deserted like Stefan had hoped. His irritation at that ceased when he looked at the middle-aged woman standing beside a fresh grave. She held a small bouquet of yellow and white flowers in her hands, along with a few tissues.

Tears streaked her face. Her chin quivered and her nose was red, not just on the tip, but almost all of it, like she'd been crying hard for a long time. Her eyes were puffy, and heavy bags hung dark beneath them.

Stefan's not-real heart plummeted. This was most likely the grave of the guy Ro had told him about. It made sense. Usually, though, the spirits arrived before the funerals—like immediately after death. Why was it that Conner had only today been greeting the newcomer?

The best way to find out was to ask Conner directly. Stefan would do that, but for now, he couldn't leave the lady to mourn by herself. It just seemed wrong. Her pain was so obvious, Stefan would swear it was permeating the air and weighing him down.

He floated closer to the woman. Her brown hair dye had faded and white shone a good inch from the roots. She wore a flowered long-sleeved shirt and dark trousers. Her hands were clenched so tightly around the bouquet that her knuckles were white.

Stefan put some thought into it and carefully brushed back a strand of hair that was in her eyes. It would feel like a breeze to her, and he needed to do something to help her.

He'd just managed to push the hair out of the way when something hit him. Stefan gasped as the air shot from his lungs. Jesus, he hadn't known there were things that could hurt him so much in the spiritual realm!

Chapter Four

He sure hadn't known there were fucking Mack trucks hanging around. Stefan held himself perfectly still, his body reacting to the trauma of being run over.

Except he hadn't been run over.

"Stay away from her!" a deep, rough voice growled in his ear.

Stefan tried to curl up into a ball. Flashbacks of the things Johnny had done to him inundated him. He whimpered, struggling to get his arms over his head. Whoever had attacked him was big, heavy, strong — and scary as any nightmare born in hell.

All this time Stefan had thought he'd been over what had happened to him. Now he knew that, better brain or not, he was still a freakin' coward.

"Shit," that voice swore gruffly, moist hot breath slicking over Stefan's skin. Images flashed by behind his closed lids. His gut cramped with remembered fear.

"Hey, kid, stop, okay?" The weight on him lifted off partially. "Seriously, stop. I'm not going to hurt you. Just don't keep crying. I'm sorry. I didn't—"

Stefan tuned out the increasingly rapidly spoken words. As soon as the man was off him enough, Stefan could *think* and he blasted the stranger with a shout that made his own ears ring. At the same time, he shot up, kicking out hard. His foot caught the man in the neck. Stefan caught a flash of startled green eyes then he was out of there.

"Stop!"

But not alone. Stefan's flight or fight impulses were fully engaged. And that had been a different voice shouting at him than the first one, which meant there were two psychotic spirits out to get him.

He wasn't a lost boy anymore, wasn't helpless or slow. He wasn't so desperate to be touched that he would let anyone hurt him.

Stefan tucked his chin to his chest and spiralled through the sky. The graveyard was long gone, and beneath him were fields and crops, farms and ranches as he headed out of town. He could feel the other two following him but didn't risk a look. If they were newly dead, his quickly hatched plan might get the two goons off his trail.

If they weren't, then Stefan wasn't averse to asking for help. Conner always did like a good fight.

Zeke Matthers and his partner Brendon's place was where Stefan was headed to. He could have just blipped himself there, as he tended to think of it. A part of him wanted a little revenge for having been tackled and terrified. Stefan shot towards the largest barn. He soared right past Zeke, who froze, having sensed him. Zeke's mama was a sweet spirit too, so Zeke probably did have some kind of ability to know when a spirit was hanging around. A sensitivity, maybe.

"Holy shit!" Brendon yelped, throwing a hand out. "Incoming!"

Stefan almost giggled at that. Brendon's eyes were huge as he shoved back a chunk of his hair. Stefan remembered when it'd still been a sandy brown instead of the mostly grey it was now.

"Oh! The pendulum!" Brendon hollered. Stefan didn't pay him any mind. He had weirdoes to shake. He turned onto his back and saw two big, muscular shapes coming up on him. Not nearly as fast as he'd gone, but they weren't slouches, either. He flipped them off and stuck out his tongue, beginning to have fun now that he wasn't being crushed.

Stefan went up twenty or thirty feet in the air, straight up. The sunlight made his eyeballs ache, but he was too scared to close his eyes. He wasn't entirely convinced the sun wouldn't turn into that Bright Light calling him away. He blinked and cursed the fact that the sun had an effect on him at all—really, he was dead! Why did his incorporeal form still react to that kind of shit?

His pursuers were rapidly catching up to him. He couldn't tell if they were furious or drooling fools thanks to the hot white spots dancing in his vision. Figuring they weren't able to see any better than he was at that point, Stefan didn't bother flipping them off again. Instead he called out to them, "Well, come on, you jerks! Pick on someone my size, you freakin' bullies!"

He didn't wait for a reaction. He bent until his hands were nearly by his ankles and shot downwards, like he was diving off a platform.

The tin roof of the barn reflected the sunlight. Stefan could hear birds and cows, regular ranch sounds, as well as Brendon's whoops of delight. A quick peek and he saw Mrs Matthers waving at him. Stefan waved back at Zeke's mom quickly. He didn't want to miss his next move. Brendon yelled something about a pendulum again but Stefan ignored him.

His stalkers were closing in on him—because Stefan was letting them. They were still going pretty fast. Stefan knew where he wanted to go. He knew exactly where he wanted *them* to go. He'd been on this ranch plenty enough times to have every bit of it memorised.

Three-quarters of the way across the barn's roof, Stefan came to a sudden stop. He'd done it often enough to be able to go from barrelling through the air to completely and utterly stopping in a flash. His pursuers, not so much. They both yelped as they shot past him. He had a flash of two pairs of green eyes, two truly magnificently muscled bodies, white-blond hair topping the head on one of them and raven-black hair on the other.

Then the two were gone, going right through the tin and wood beneath it. That told Stefan they weren't very experienced. He dipped his head down through the roofing material just in time to see both men land in the dirty stall. It'd have been better if they'd had a corporeal body, but landing in horse shit wasn't pleasant in any form.

Stefan lit out of there, laughing his ass off as he went. He should have remembered that cockiness was a sure-fire temptation karma never could resist.

He knew the second steely arms wrapped around his calves that he should have just popped on home instead of taking to the air. Stefan pictured his room, his nice bed that he loved even though he didn't really need it, the laptop and all the pictures Lee had set out for him.

"Jo, grab onto me!"

Stefan heard the order even as he dissipated from the air. If those two bozos thought they were going with him, they were wrong. Blipping didn't work that way.

His room was just as he'd left it. Stefan sighed and flopped onto the pretty blue and green blanket topping the bed. He stared up at the white ceiling, tense, doubting what he believed to be a truth. When his pursuers didn't appear after a few minutes, he relaxed and exhaled noisily.

"What a weird day." Stefan tucked his hands behind his head. He wondered where Conner was. Later he'd find him and tell him about the two aggressive spirits. Conner would run them off.

And Stefan was back to being bored. A nap sounded like the way to go, so he closed his eyes and let sleep take him away for a while.

* * * *

Confused didn't even begin to cover how Gideon felt. Jordan wore a stunned expression that probably matched the one on Gideon's face.

"How did that little shit do all of that?" Jordan groused. "If that horse shit had really gotten on us, I'd have to find the kid and put him over my knee."

"I did attack him first," Gideon pointed out. "I'm actually kind of impressed. He out-manoeuvred us."

"Because we don't know how to be what we are!" Jordan exclaimed, tossing his hands up. "That Conner guy wasn't exactly helpful with his welcome home speech. I don't even remember what he said."

Gideon didn't either. They'd both been distracted by the arrival of Jordan's casket for the burial.

"Where did he go?" Jordan continued. "Conner said we could go from one place to the other, but we tried that after we died, and look how long it took us to get to McKinton!"

It had definitely been hit and miss with them. *Mostly miss,* Gideon scoffed silently. "We were able to get here, we just took the scenic route. It's not like we were tired or starving. We got here just fine, and we saw a helluva lot of the world."

"I hate not eating," Jordan muttered. "I want to eat. I loved food. I miss it."

Gideon nodded, but he could take it or leave it. He'd always eaten because his body had needed the nutrition. It didn't really matter now.

"Sex!" Jordan yelped, his eyes positively huge as he sputtered. He finally got a sentence out. "I'm never going to have sex again!"

"Why not?" Gideon asked, moving over to his friend. He put a hand on Jordan's crotch and squeezed his junk.

"Or maybe I will," Jordan rasped, tipping his head back. "More, Gid? I know we said before, we wouldn't touch each other, but now…"

"Before, we were both alive and unwilling to risk damaging our friendship. That didn't keep us from fucking guys together." Gideon massaged the hardening length under his palm. Jo had a nice, thick cock. If Gideon were the type of guy who liked to get fucked, he'd be all over it. Hell, if he could even tolerate a dick up his ass he'd stick that big shaft up there.

However, he didn't like getting fucked. At all. He'd tried it with guys who'd known what they were doing, and it just didn't get him off. Jo was a top, too, but that didn't mean they couldn't still have some fun together.

"You know we're still in the air?" Jo huffed.

Gideon shrugged. "So? We aren't going anywhere, and there's the matter of this…" He ran his thumb over the tip of Jo's cock.

"Ah, God." Jo shuddered and quickly worked his pants open. His cock popped right out, heavy and hot where it touched Gideon's skin.

"Nice," Gideon murmured as he took Jo's shaft in hand. "Push your pants down past your balls, too. Give it all to me."

"I don't bottom, you know that," Jo snapped, but he didn't sound quite so firm about it.

Gideon filed that information away for later. When they'd been serving their country in the Marines, they'd immediately been drawn to each other. It had taken a little bit of talking and not so subtle hints for each of them to figure out the other was gay. Then they'd both confessed to being tops. After a laugh over that, they had settled on being friends who shared when they could, because finding a guy to fuck in the desert could be damned hard to do at times.

"We kept our hands off each other all that time," Gideon murmured as he studied the contrast of his darkly tanned hand against Jo's pink and plum cock. "Not even doing this for each other." Gideon palmed Jo's balls and gave them a slight squeeze while at the same time stroking his cock. "We were idiots."

"Yeah, we were," Jordan said in a strained voice. "Fuck, I hadn't even thought about coming until…until…"

"Until you freaked out thinking you'd never come again," Gideon finished as he gave another couple of up-and-down moves, pumping Jo's dick. "But you're gonna come for me, aren't you?"

"For me," Jo muttered stubbornly. "You're not my top."

"Maybe not." Gideon leaned close until he had his lips right on the delicate curve of Jo's ear. "But maybe I will be. Would you like that, Jo? Like for me to fuck you?"

"I—" Jo gasped and reached up to pinch at his own tits. "Oh God, fuck! Don't bottom," he got out.

"So you said." But Gideon could see it, the need in Jo's eyes, the hunger there before they glazed over. "We were both playing it safe. I think maybe you like the idea of me fucking you. Have you ever been fucked?"

Jo didn't answer, not verbally anyway. His cock pulsed and hot cum jetted from it. Gideon massaged his length through the climax, then he bent down and licked the sticky stuff off his hands.

With that cleaned up, he then lapped at the glistening liquid on the crown of Jo's shaft.

"Fuck," Jo dragged out repeatedly while Gideon gently suckled his softening cock. Jo's spunk had a burnt, almost bitter taste to it. Gideon liked it, a lot.

"No fucking me," Jo said a few moments later when he grabbed Gideon by the hair. "I don't have to try slicing off my own arm to know I wouldn't like that. I don't need to be fucked to know I don't like it, either."

Gideon released Jo's cock with a wet sound. He looked into Jo's green eyes. Jo's eyelashes were tipped with blond, almost white, like the hair on his head and at his groin. The man was sexy as sin and he knew it.

He was also dead wrong in his way of thinking. "Even I tried it a few times before deciding anal sex wasn't for me—not if it meant being on the receiving end, at least. It's not something you should rule out if you haven't done it enough to be sure you hate it."

Jo narrowed his eyes. "Really. And just how many times did it take you to figure it out?"

Gideon held up one hand. "I gave it a shot five times, with a few different guys. All of them were good with the prepping and all of that. Just didn't do anything for me to have them fuck me." He shrugged. "I wish it did, but I hated it every single time. I'd still suggest you try it before swearing off of it."

"Let me guess." Jo crossed his arms over his chest. "You'd be willing to make the sacrifice and be the one to fuck me?"

Gideon shot up until he was almost nose to nose with Jo. "Don't try to make me into a dick. I'd love to fuck that ass of yours, sure, but not at the expense of our friendship. If you think that's all I'm after, then—"

"I don't," Jo said, cutting him off. "Look, let me think about it, okay? I don't know that I'll ever want to try it, but maybe you're right. Lots of guys sure have enjoyed having a dick in their ass. A lot. I might, too."

"Maybe." Gideon was still a little hurt but he let the matter drop. They were both having to adjust to an entirely new reality.

"You need some relief?" Jo asked.

Gideon shook his head. His erection had waned when the talking had gone to shit. "Nope. I can wait. We should go back to check on your mom."

Jo shivered and rubbed his arms. "I don't want to. I can't handle seeing it, knowing…"

Well, Gideon actually understood that. He didn't know where the bits and pieces of his dead body were, but there'd be no one to claim him. His parents had died of drug overdoses a long time ago. There'd been no extended family, either.

Gideon examined his friend. Jo looked like he was close to bolting, and Gideon didn't want that. If something happened and they were separated they might never find each other again.

"We could go search for the kid," he suggested, even though he was certain the 'kid' was anything but a child. That'd been an adult man glaring at him and Jo, and it'd been a firm, mature sexy male body under Gideon's when he'd tackled the stranger. "He was interesting."

"He was cute even with the attitude," Jo agreed. "Maybe we can entice him to the dark side." The seductive smile on Jo's handsome face would have brought anyone over to their side, in Gideon's opinion. The man was too good-looking for his own good. Gideon had always thought so, but since they'd both declared themselves tops, he'd left that train of thought alone.

But now he'd actually given Jo a hand job and had sucked his dick, tasted his cream. Gideon wanted more. The face of the kid—*no, the man*—that he'd tackled flashed before his eyes. The man had thick, wild brown hair with fat curls making it look pettable. Large brown eyes framed with thick lashes, a short, slightly upturned nose and plump mauve lips, all on a face that could have been sculpted by the finest artist in the world.

"He was actually better than cute," Jo mumbled.

Gideon snapped out of his musings and frowned at his friend. "Can you read my mind?"

Jo snorted. "Of course not. I was lost in my own thoughts about the guy."

Gideon could understand that. "All right. You want to find him?"

"I—" Jo stopped and tipped his head back, examining the sky. His Adam's apple bobbed when he swallowed. He angled his head down again and met Gideon's stare with his own. "I need to check on Mom, you're right about that. Maybe she's not in the graveyard anymore. We can start at the house. After that, I'm all for finding that whirlwind who dumped us in the stall."

"We dumped ourselves there," Gideon pointed out.

Jo hitched up one shoulder. "Semantics. He knew we didn't have a clue how to stop like he did, and he sure as shit knew where we'd be landing."

"Ha ha," Gideon grumbled over the 'sure as shit' part of that.

"I want to know how him and Conner do that popping away sort of thing. Teleporting, or whatever it is." Jo nodded. "Yup, need to know that, and to find out how to do it, we need to talk to the slippery stud who got away."

"Or Conner," Gideon said. "He'd know how."

Jo wiggled one finger back and forth. "No, no, no. We're going to find that sexy man and have him explain it to us."

Gideon saw a flaw with that logic. "He'll probably just disappear on us again if we find him."

"Not if I beg pretty enough, he won't. I hope." Jo smirked. "Think I can get him to hear us out?"

"With that smug grin, you can probably have the guy naked and bent over in two seconds flat," Gideon informed him.

Jo laughed and rubbed his hands together before reaching to pull his pants back up. "Well, all right then, there's even more incentive to find him now!"

Chapter Five

Jordan was still rattled by being dead and not so dead. *Dead and a spirit. How does that even happen?* Conner had been a friendly enough guy, and insistent that they be called spirits not ghosts. Jordan kind of thought that was because everyone would then be referring to Conner as Conner the friendly ghost. Somehow he was pretty certain that would irk Conner. Jordan couldn't think of a logical reason for them not to be called ghosts, but he supposed it didn't matter in the end — he was still dead.

He sneaked a peek at Gideon. The big, growly soldier had been a solid friend, and they'd had good times together. Jordan had kept his crush on Gideon buried deep inside. Having Gideon touch him earlier had been a culmination of some seriously repressed fantasies.

It'd been fucking perfect. Gideon's grip had been firm and rough, but not painfully so. He had a confidence about him that was sexier than it should have been. Jordan had worked hard to keep from ever making any kind of a sexual move on Gid, but now that line had been crossed. Chances were good it'd keep on being crossed.

And he knew, though he wasn't about to 'fess up to Gid, that he'd let Gideon fuck him. Just not yet. Jordan liked Gid, respected him, thought he was a stud. He still wasn't eager to offer up his ass to the guy.

Now, the idea of finding the sexy fucker who'd left them behind, that was intriguing. Jordan's cock was hard again just thinking of the man. He'd never recovered so quickly from such an intense orgasm before. Maybe being dead imbued him with super-dick powers or something. The laws of a living man's refractory period certainly weren't applicable to him, not now. *Good. Being a spirit should have some bonuses.*

Jordan wasn't sure why he was still on Earth. He'd been hurting so bad, and yeah, he'd been scared, knowing he was dying, knowing he was alone. Then he'd seen Gid floating above him. Hope had chased away some of the fear, and when Jordan had died, he'd gone to the man he'd fought side by side with during the last two tours. It only seemed right that they stay together.

"Seeing Mom almost killed me all over again," Jordan said to Gideon as he floated beside him. That was more emotional than anything Jordan might have ever admitted to in his former life, but he just didn't see the point in keeping it in now. He was dead, for Christ's sake. Maybe that meant he didn't have to be such a rigid guy.

Gideon reached out and patted him on the shoulder. "She'll be okay. She has that guy she's dating to help her, so at least she's not alone. Plus the whole town seemed to show up for your funeral."

"Yeah," Jordan mumbled. He didn't ask Gideon if he regretted coming with Jordan. He didn't want to hear it if he did, not yet at least. Gideon didn't have any family to mourn him, and Jordan couldn't imagine it'd be a good thing for Gideon to go off and brood about. They needed to be there in McKinton together.

"She's not at the graveyard," Gideon told him as they neared it.

"Thanks for checking." Jordan didn't know if he'd ever be able to stand there and look down at his grave. It was fucking creepy seeing it. "Let's swing by the house."

"No need." Gideon pointed when Jordan glanced at him. "She's in the parking lot with Craig."

"Craig." Jordan wasn't sure how he felt about the man his mother seemed to be in love with. "She hasn't dated anyone seriously in…ever. At least not since she got knocked up with me."

"Your old man take off?" Gideon asked. "You've never mentioned him."

Jordan watched Craig help his mother into the truck. "Nah, he died. Killed himself, Mom said. He had problems."

"Sounds like it," Gideon agreed. "Still, I'm sorry."

"Thanks." Jordan hovered in the air about ten feet off the ground. It was so bizarre to see himself doing that. Almost as strange as it was to look over and see Gideon suspended in air. "I wonder how we go about finding Conner? He has to know who the guy is we're trying to find."

"Seems like it." Gideon put a hand above his eyes, shielding them from the sun. "I guess we just start popping in places."

"I heard my name spoken."

"Jesus fucking—" Jordan spun around as he slapped a hand to his chest. "If I wasn't already dead…"

Conner snickered and gave him a thumbs up. Gideon was still cussing.

"Seriously, Conner. What are you, a genie?"

"A genie?" Conner stopped chortling long enough to ask Jordan.

Jordan didn't have a good explanation. Didn't stop him from trying. "You just pop up out of nowhere because you heard your name spoken? What else could do that?"

"Me," Conner said. "Except I really didn't. I came back to see if you were still stunned stupid by seeing your own burial. It was just my good fortune that I got to sneak up on you, too."

"He does that a lot," another man said as he materialised out of thin air.

Jordan just barely kept from squeaking. Gideon cussed again. The newcomer was lithe and beautiful, with shiny black hair and finely chiselled cheekbones.

"He's mine," Conner said companionably. "But I can't blame you for looking at Ro. He's perfect, isn't he?"

Ro's honey-brown skin darkened over his cheekbones, but he turned a pleased smile on Conner. "Flatterer."

"Honest," Conner countered with as he looped an arm around Ro's shoulders. "Ro, this is Jordan, and the cussing wonder is Gideon."

"Hey." Ro waved. "Sorry to meet y'all like this. Did either of you happen to see a guy here earlier, cute and slender, dark curly hair? Stefan? His name is Stefan."

"Stefan." Just saying the man's name made Jordan horny. "We didn't meet him, exactly, at least not the traditional way. Not at first."

It shouldn't have been possible for a spirit to look so intimidating, considering they were all already dead. What else could happen to them? Yet the expression on Conner's face surely could strike fear into the heart of any being.

"I kind of tackled him," Gideon admitted.

"Kind of?" Conner repeated in a soft tone that somehow projected his turn from friendly to fierce immediately.

Jordan suddenly had a very bad feeling that they were in deep shit. "He—"

Before he could get another word out, the air around him seemed to tighten. It wasn't possible for air to grow dense and heavy like cement walls pushing him on all sides—but it was happening. Gideon's open-mouthed, stunned look told Jordan that he was experiencing it too.

"You do *not* fuck with Stefan," Jordan heard Conner say right before everything went dark.

Almost as suddenly as that happened, it was light again. Jordan blinked in confusion. They were in a room he didn't recognise, and Conner was there, along with the pretty man, Ro.

More importantly, there was another man in the room. Stefan frowned at Jordan and Gideon before turning a fierce look on Conner. "Why in the *world* did you bring these two bullies here?"

Jordan still felt restricted—almost completely. He tried to speak but Conner held a hand up and spared him a cold glance.

"One, I wanted to make sure you're okay—"

"What're they gonna do to me?" Stefan interrupted, huffing slightly. "I'm already dead."

"You can still be hurt," Conner explained, and the invisible bands around Jordan tightened. "What happened?"

Stefan examined Jordan and Gideon each for a moment before turning back to Conner. "What're you doing to them?"

Conner shrugged. "What happened?"

Stefan planted two large, bony hands on his hips. "First I want to know how you're doing that, and what you're doing."

Conner sighed like he was the most put-upon man ever in existence. "Stef, now's really not the time to explain either of those things. I mean, Jordan and Gideon are both right here and listening to everything we say."

Stefan spared them another glance. "Yeah, well, can't you plug their ears or something?"

Jordan sputtered almost as loudly as Gideon did, not wanting Conner to be fucking around with his hearing.

Conner ignored them. "Nope. I'm not a god, despite how sexy I am." He buffed the nails of one hand on his chest then examined them. "I can see where anyone might think so—ouch!" he yelped when Ro popped him on the back of the head.

"Quit tormenting everyone."

Conner snapped a smart salute to Ro and winked at him. "Yessir." Then he pointed at Jordan and Gideon. "Try anything funny and I'll have you both bottled up and tossed into the ocean."

"You can do that?" Stefan asked excitedly.

Conner's lips thinned. Jordan took that as a no, but he wasn't going to test it.

"Seriously, can you?" Stefan asked again. "Because if you can, you have to share the how of it just like you have to tell me what you were doing to them." He jabbed a thumb towards Jordan. "You can't keep all that knowledge to yourself, it's just not fair."

Conner arched an eyebrow at Stefan. "Gonna stomp your foot, too?"

Stefan cocked a hip. "Maybe."

"Children," Ro said sharply. "Behave."

Conner and Stefan both broke into chuckles. "Fine," Conner said. "Later, Stef. I won't talk about it in front of anyone other than you and Ro."

"Deal." Stefan pivoted around and marched right up to Gideon. "I had enough of being bullied when I was alive."

Gideon's cheeks turned ruddy. Jordan was sure his did, too.

"I thought you were going to hurt Jo's mom," Gideon muttered.

Stefan looked at them both like they were crazy. "Why would I do that?"

"I don't know," Gideon answered as he turned his hands palms up in front of him. "I've been fighting in Afghanistan for the past two years. I just got killed by a suicide bomber. Forgive me for being jumpy and suspicious."

Stefan seemed to shrink a little as he stepped back. "Well, I feel like an ass."

"I don't." Conner glared at Gideon.

"It's okay, Conner." Stefan gestured at Conner, a sort of wave as if he was shooing off Conner's ire. "Seriously, I guess I can understand, and I did lead them out to Zeke and Brendon's for a dunk in the shitty stall."

Conner's laughter rang out as he held up a hand.

Stefan high-fived him. "It'd have been better if they'd gone solid when they hit, though."

Jordan cleared his throat. He was guessing he could speak now without incurring Conner's wrath. "How would we do that, the go solid thing?" He looked around the room. "And how do we just appear somewhere else?"

Conner narrowed his eyes at Jordan. "If either of you ever fuck around with Stefan again, you'll regret it."

"We won't," Jordan assured him, wondering what, exactly, Stefan was to Conner. The big blond spirit was certainly protective of Stefan. "We aren't assholes. We just don't know anything about any of this." He waved a hand around the room in general. "One minute we were alive, then Gid was dead and I was dying. Then we were both dead, and confused. It took us a week to get here, and now I'm thinking we could have probably gotten here a hell of a lot quicker."

"Yup," Stefan said before Conner even got his mouth opened. "You sure could have. All you do is—"

"Stefan," Conner growled.

Stefan didn't even acknowledge Conner. "Think of where you want to be. It's hard at first, but you kind of picture it, or the idea of it if wherever you're going isn't somewhere you've actually seen. And don't freak out if you appear in a wall or a sidewalk. It's not like you're stuck, you know. You just float out of it."

"I was going to explain it," Conner was whispering to Ro. "I wasn't going to be mean."

"The firming up is harder," Stefan continued. "We can touch each other." Stefan's smile was devastating as he approached Jordan. He placed his hand right over Jordan's heart, which fluttered wildly. "See? No problem. And you can touch me, too."

Stefan used his other hand to grab Jordan's right wrist. "Like this." Jordan sucked in a noisy breath when he felt the warmth of Stefan's body through his clothes. Stefan was slight of build, but he wasn't too thin, and he was simply gorgeous with those big eyes and that trusting expression.

"Are you—" Conner broke off with a grunt. "What, Ro?"

Stefan used the hand he'd grabbed Jordan's wrist with to touch Gideon's chest. Jordan knew the ticking at the joint of Gideon's jaw was a sign of arousal. He'd seen it before.

"But touching another spirit is different from touching something more…" Stefan pulled his hands back and rolled his eyes up to stare at the ceiling as he seemed to search for a word. Finally he looked at them again. "Something more substantial, for lack of a better word. We only have substance here, in our afterlife, not in the real world that the living are in. It's weird, but what can you do?" He hitched a shoulder up and let it drop. "It is what it is. You have to really concentrate to have an effect on things. If you don't want to fall through a barn roof, for example, you just concentrate on not doing that."

"Think *stop*," Ro said. "Envision yourself doing it."

"Instead of panicking," Conner added. "See?" He turned to Ro. "I can be helpful."

"Conner says it gets easier to do the more you practise," Stefan said. He moved over to his laptop and tapped a button. Porn music blared as a raunchy video began playing.

"Seriously?" someone hollered from another room. "Turn it down!"

"Whoops. Forgot about the volume." Stefan tapped a button and the sound was turned off.

Conner shot over to get between Stefan and the laptop. "Don't stop the video on our account. I haven't seen this one before."

"Why don't we watch it somewhere more private?" Ro asked, gliding over to press up against Conner's side. "Now that you know Stefan's okay, and these two weren't trying to hurt him."

Conner gave Jordan and Gideon a stern look before looping an arm around Stefan's neck and knuckling his hair. "They give you any shit, holler."

"I will." Stefan giggled and slipped out of Conner's grasp. "Have fun."

Ro hugged Stefan. "You, don't have too much fun."

"I'm not a kid," Stefan said gruffly.

Jordan warmed up inside. He knew he was probably reading more into Ro's words and Stefan's reply than he should, but Stefan was a sexy young man and Jordan…

Jordan couldn't affirm that he was still alive by having rough, mind-blowing sex, but he could remind himself that at least he and Gideon weren't completely gone.

Chapter Six

Maybe he was being presumptuous, but Stefan was pretty damned sure that'd been lust he'd seen in Jordan's eyes. Gideon, he couldn't read, but Jordan had this hungry look about him, and now that he knew neither of them was out to harm him, Stefan could admit they were both gorgeous.

Not model-perfect, but rough paragons of masculinity that made Stefan want to drop and worship at their feet. These weren't boys, either, like Johnny had been. No, Gideon and Jordan were grown men, with more experiences in their too-short lives than Stefan could ever hope to have.

Both men had darkly tanned skin, and crow's feet spreading from the outer corners of their eyes. Gideon had a single shallow line running almost fully across his forehead. Jordan had two thin ones right in the centre of his brow.

They looked hard, lived-in and sexier than anyone else Stefan had ever seen. Jordan watched him with something that Stefan could only describe as hunger.

He peeked at Gideon. Nope, he couldn't read that man's expression at all.

"What do you think, Gid?" Jordan asked, never looking away from Stefan. He reached down and adjusted his cock. Stefan wanted to offer to do it for him, but that was more forward than he could be just then. He'd flirted, touched both men, then flicked on the porn just to see if he got a hit on either being gay. He knew Jordan was, at least. Gay, and interested.

Gideon didn't answer, but he watched Stefan steadily.

Stefan cleared his throat and ran his fingers through his hair. He felt warm, flushed and aroused but above all of that, he experienced a sudden surge of trepidation. Something was going on that he couldn't quite grasp and that he wasn't ready for after all.

He looked over at Gideon then flicked his gaze to Jordan. "I, um. Have to—" Stefan didn't know what to do with his hands. They seemed to be fluttering in front of him all of their own accord. Damn, he was nervous. "Gotta go. Feel free to watch the video."

Stefan whirled around and would have left had Gideon not decided to speak.

"Wait, please."

Oh damn. Stefan's cock was hard as a steel girder as soon as Gideon spoke.

"Jordan and I didn't mean to make you uncomfortable," Gideon said in a softer voice. "Just like I didn't mean to be a jerk earlier. I just saw a spirit hovering over Jo's mom, and I freaked. I tend to be protective of wounded people."

The woman had been in so much pain. That was one of the reasons why Stefan hadn't been able to resist touching her hair.

"He's also protective of his friends." Jordan had a slightly higher-pitched voice, but it was every bit as stimulating at the moment as Gideon's. "I wasn't handling the whole seeing my own grave thing very well, and my mom, Jesus, that's the hardest thing I've ever had to see, her sobbing over my casket."

Stefan forgot about his hard-on, and about his raging hormones that kept telling him he wanted to get fucked then petering out before he could go through with it. Jordan's words penetrated his own selfish musings and wants, calling him out on them as shallow, vain worries of an immature youth. Despite his age, Stefan wasn't as mature as he'd thought.

He set aside everything having to do with him and moved to stand in front of Gideon and Jordan, who were shoulder to shoulder. "I'm sorry," Stefan got out past a lump in his throat.

"For what?" Jordan asked, sounding genuinely confused.

Stefan forced himself to look both men in the eyes, though he felt like he was watching a tennis match, bouncing his gaze back and forth between them. "I'm sorry that you both died. I'm sorry that you"—he tipped his chin at Jordan—"had to see your mother torn up over your death. At least she loves you, and *that* is a big, big thing. I'm even sorry about earlier, kind of."

"Kind of?"

Stefan looked at Gideon and couldn't quite keep from smiling. "I had fun out-manoeuvring you both. I mean, come on. Y'all are these big"—he raked them both over visually—"strong, masculine guys who just exude sex appeal."

"We do?" Jordan asked.

Gideon snorted and stood a little taller. "I do."

Jordan smacked his shoulder. "Not."

"You both do," Stefan clarified before they could start really bickering. "Y'all are sex on a stick, even though I don't know what the hell that means. It doesn't make sense, so maybe I should say y'all are the sexiest fuckers I've ever seen." Stefan wished he could take the admission back. Fear tingled along his spine as he moved back several feet.

Jordan and Gideon glanced at each other then both looked at him. Gideon eased somehow, making himself look not so big and burly. "You're sending some seriously mixed signals, you know that, right?"

Stefan nodded. "Yeah. Sorry for that, too."

"You're gay?" Jordan asked.

Stefan giggled and pointed to the still-running video. "Uh, yeah."

Jordan paled a little. "Virgin?" Stefan frowned. "I mean, are you a virgin?" Jordan clarified.

"Well, I figured that's what you mean," Stefan grumbled. "I just didn't want you to ask me."

"So you are," Jordan assumed.

Stefan held up one finger and moved it from side to side. "Ah-ah. Don't go trying to jump a whole river when there's just a puddle in front of you."

Gideon snickered but Jordan grimaced. "What do you mean?"

"I mean—" God help him, he had to say it but the words sure didn't want to come out. "I'm not a virgin," he got out, but his voice broke and he had flashbacks to the hell that was puberty. "I've been fucked before." And he was torn between wanting to be again, and running off to hide in a dark spot somewhere.

"While you were alive, or after?" Gideon asked.

Stefan stopped being fearful and glared at Gideon. "What, it can't have been both?"

Gideon didn't seem to be the least bit intimidated. "Sure, but you're running hot and cold." Then he widened his eyes slightly. "Oh."

"Oh what?" Stefan scowled at Gideon. What the hell was the guy's problem?

Gideon nodded. "I get it, then. You're attracted to Jordan, but not me. Don't worry, it's not a 'both of us or neither' kind of deal."

"It isn't?" Jordan turned to face Gideon fully.

Gideon bit his bottom lip.

Stefan regarded both men. Something was happening between them, obviously. No one was volunteering anything either. There was no helping it, he'd have to ask if he wanted to know what was going on. "Are you two a couple?"

"Not exactly," Jordan said at the same time that Gideon stated, "No."

The two soldiers glared at each other.

"Y'all might want to get that figured out," Stefan told them, amused and disappointed at the same time. He wasn't going to come between a couple, or an almost-couple.

Jordan finally turned back to meet Stefan's gaze. "We've messed around with guys together before, but hadn't ever touched one another sexually until earlier today. It's—" He shook his head. "Gid's right. We're not a couple, but we're buddies in ways that might not go over so well with a potential lover." Jordan lowered his eyelids, a sultry expression sliding into place. "Unless, of course, that lover was willing to be ours instead of just mine or Gideon's."

Holy—talk about every slut wannabe's fantasies! Stefan's poor dick was going to be sore as hell from rapidly deflating and filling repeatedly. His emotions kept sliding all over the place, and the conversation hadn't been constantly sexual enough to keep his shaft erect.

"He looks scared," Jordan murmured.

"Doesn't mean my ears quit working," Stefan snapped. He hated that they could see his fear. "I…" Boy, he was a brilliant conversationalist. Stefan tried again. "I don't understand what you're saying, exactly." And it made him feel dumb again, which in turn made him angry at himself. "Never mind."

"Can I kiss you?" Jordan asked, the question stopping Stefan from bolting, it shocked him so much.

"Huh?" he managed but other than that, he was stumped.

Jordan came closer until Stefan could see the dozens of flecks of grey in his eyes. "Can I kiss you?" he repeated.

Stefan's heart had done a magic trick. It'd gone and turned into a hummingbird. At least, that was how it felt to him when he pressed a hand over it. "What about Gideon?"

Jordan's smile lit all kinds of needy fires in Stefan. "Yeah, you can kiss him too. He'd like that."

"Not if Stefan wouldn't like it," Gideon added quickly.

Jordan reached out slowly, so slowly that Stefan had the opportunity to escape a dozen times before Jordan's hand cupped his cheek. "I've never kissed Gid, Stefan. I bet he tastes good."

Stefan gulped and tried not to sway forward, but Jordan was drawing him in with that seductive voice and the feel of his palm against Stefan's skin. Stefan licked his lips and noticed that Jordan licked his too. Did that mean they were going to kiss? What about

Gideon? Stefan couldn't help but sneak a peek at the other man.

"Damn," he whispered when his gaze tangled with Gideon's. There was such need coming from him. Stefan didn't think it was all for Jordan, either, though there were some kind of feelings between the two men. But Gideon wanted him, wanted Stefan enough that it was obvious to Stefan.

"Mm, that's what I think, too. Just, damn, look at Gid." Jordan turned to watch the other man along with Stefan.

Stefan wanted to kiss Gideon, he wanted to kiss Jordan—*Hell, maybe I just want to kiss everyone!* Except he didn't. *Only Gideon and Jordan have lit me up with lust like this.*

Stefan didn't know how to make the next move. He thought he'd have to be the one to do something more because Gideon and Jordan had already put some of themselves on the line.

That was easier to think about than to actually do. Stefan felt frozen in place, held under a spell of lust and fear that he wasn't sure he liked. The fear, at least. He hated that particular emotion.

Gideon came closer and Stefan's pulse raced. "I want—" He reached out with one hand. The words were too hard to form when his mouth had started watering.

Gideon took his hand, and something that might have been tenderness flitted across his features. "Does this mean you want me to kiss you?"

Stefan nodded, unable to articulate an answer.

"And Jordan, do you want him to kiss you, too?"

Stefan bobbed his head again. He wanted those kisses, and so much more. *Maybe.*

Then his brain shut down its worrying because Gideon pulled him into his strong arms and before Stefan could blink he was being kissed with a passion he'd only dreamt of experiencing.

Stefan moaned and closed his eyes as he clung to Gideon. He tried to keep up, to suck and lick, to twist and turn his tongue and do everything Gideon was doing to him. It just wasn't possible. Stefan didn't have experience kissing. Gideon mastered him in seconds, and Stefan loved it.

He felt safe and wanted in Gideon's arms. Stefan hadn't even realised he'd felt unsafe until then. Gideon nipped his bottom lip and Stefan forgot everything but the taste and feel of the man.

Until Gideon gentled the kiss and finally raised his head. "Jordan," Gideon said in a rough voice.

And Stefan was being handed over and kissed again. It was another world-rocking kiss, although Jordan's was different. He wasn't as dominating, and Stefan liked that as much as he'd liked Gideon's rigid control.

"Beautiful," he heard Gideon murmur just before the kiss changed, becoming messy and wet, perfect and awkward as Gideon joined in.

Stefan grabbed a handful of each man's shirt. He needed to in order to anchor himself in place, or else he was surely going to float right off into space. He was so turned on and so happy, it was almost incomprehensible.

Gideon made a rumbling, growly sound as he nibbled at Stefan's lip. Someone—again, Gideon, Stefan thought—slid a hand over Stefan's dick. Even through his clothes, the touch burnt with an erotic power that was addictive.

Stefan jerked as his cock pulsed and he came. Maybe he should have been embarrassed about shooting so quickly, but he was too euphoric to care.

"Shit, he smells so good," Jordan rasped. Stefan opened one eye just enough to see out. Jordan was watching him and jerking Gideon off.

Stefan came out of his orgasm-haze instantly. He opened his other eye and gaped at the big dick Jordan was jacking. Damn, but Gideon was hung. He had a big, thick cock with a wide-slitted crown. As Stefan watched, cum jetted from the tip.

"Owed you one," Jordan said, then he jerked Gideon's face to his with a grip to Gideon's nape. Stefan enjoyed the way the two men kissed each other. It was more like a battle of wills with not even a hint of tenderness in it.

Gideon reached out but Stefan scooted away. "No. I want to watch." For one thing, he wasn't about to risk Gideon wanting to fuck him. Even if he kind of wanted him to. But Gideon's dick was a lot bigger than Johnny's, and Jordan's probably was too. Considering how bad it'd hurt when Johnny had fucked him, Stefan was going to seriously have to rethink the whole anal-sex desire he kept having.

Gideon pushed Jordan back and both men were partially obscured by the bed. Stefan sighed internally. He was definitely going to have to teach them how not to blend in with everything.

For now, however, he could see them from mid-thigh up. That was good enough.

Jordan and Gideon scrambled to get each other's clothes off. Stefan's cock twitched and he removed his clothes with a thought. He fisted his shaft, shivering at how good it felt to do so. That sensitive length was even harder after two strokes.

Gideon snarled and ripped Jordan's shirt off. They scuffled then the remains of their clothes were gone in an instant, one or both of them having put enough thought into getting them naked.

Jordan leant back and if he'd been a living being, he'd have fallen over, but he wasn't and Gideon was on him almost before Stefan could admire the sheer beauty of both men's naked forms.

There was no way he could miss the fat cock Jordan had been blessed with, either. Stefan looked down at his own dick and frowned. He'd never felt insecure about his size there before, but now he wondered.

A moan drew his attention off his own potential shortcomings. Gideon was sucking on Jordan's neck, marking him from the looks of it. Stefan floated over them so he could have a better view of the happenings. Jordan's eyes rolled back in his head when Gideon pinched both of his dusky brown nipples.

Gideon rumbled wordlessly then proceeded to lick and suck his way down to Jordan's cock. Jordan panted and grabbed at Gideon's head, but his dark hair was too short to hang onto.

Jordan pawed at the air then managed to rest his hands on Gideon's broad shoulders. Stefan gasped when Gideon sucked the entire length of Jordan's shaft into his mouth. Jordan shouted and Gideon bobbed back up and rubbed his lips over Jordan's crown.

"Fuck! Gid, please—"

Stefan wasn't sure what Jordan was begging for, but Gideon sucked his cock down again and Jordan began thrusting immediately. He let go of one shoulder and reached to twist his own nipple again. Stefan mimicked the move on himself, plucking at his own nipples. He watched the way Gideon's ass moved as he humped against Jordan's leg. Before Stefan could stop himself, he came closer and ran a hand down the length of Gideon's back, all the way down to his rock-hard ass.

Gideon began to thrust harder. Stefan jacked himself at a similar speed as he traced small patterns on Gideon's buttocks. The light coating of hair on his rump was irresistible. It was soft and crinkly at the same time. When Gideon pushed his hips up, it brought his buttock firmly against Stefan's palm. Stefan liked that too and after a minute or two, he dared to drag his fingernails over that sexy backside.

Gideon shook like he was coming apart. Stefan thought at first that he'd done something wrong, then he realised that no, he hadn't. Gideon was climaxing again, and Jordan was too, wispy hints of breaths slipping from his lips as he frantically fucked Gideon's mouth.

Stefan's balls tingled and drew up as he watched the other two men come. They were so gorgeous, so rough and hungry for each other. Then Jordan's gaze met his, and Stefan knew in that instant that it wasn't just Gideon that Jordan wanted.

Stefan threw his head back and in trying to keep from whimpering with the pleasure overwhelming him, ended up making an embarrassingly gurgly sound as his orgasm peaked. He pumped out several jets of cum and heard Gideon hiss after the last trickle was released.

"Stefan."

Gideon's voice was rough as old asphalt. Stefan trembled upon hearing it. He tipped his head back down and bit his lip when he saw where his jizz had landed. He couldn't look away from his essence on

Gideon's back and buttocks. There, especially, it was tangled in that black fuzz Stefan had admired moments before. One splotch of the stuff had even landed dead centre in Gideon's crack.

"Sorry," he finally made himself say but he couldn't drag his gaze away from the sexy sight.

"No you're not," Gideon countered. "And neither am I. I just want to know, who's gonna clean it off of me?"

Chapter Seven

The cooling gobs of spunk vanished as soon as Gideon had asked the question. He frowned and tried to get a better look at his own butt. "How'd you do that?" he asked Stefan.

"I just did it, like I just do this." Stefan was clothed again, covering entirely too much of his delectable body. "I wanted to be covered up in my favourite clothes, so I am. Same with the, er, the mess I made."

"This is all very interesting," Jordan interjected in a strained voice. "But I want to know how, even as a spirit, I can need a damn nap so bad I want to scream."

"I don't know how a lot of things work," Stefan said, settling down on the bed, the mattress actually sinking under his weight just a few inches. "I sleep, too. I think we all do, except maybe not Conner. Not much, anyway. Is it a remembered need from when we were alive? Why do we breathe, and are we really breathing?" Stefan shrugged. "Whatever, we keep doing it. I quit questioning most of it because it'd drive me crazy if I didn't."

"How do we learn to do the stuff you do?" Gideon gestured to where Stefan sat. "Can you feel the bed?"

Stefan nodded. "Yeah, just barely. If I completely forget to keep in mind that I need to stay more substantial, I'll look up and realise I'm up to my chest in mattress. No big deal if that happens, but I like to feel stuff when I can." Stefan scrunched up his face in a way that made him look more innocent than he was, considering what they'd all just done. "Actually, I don't even think about it subconsciously now. It's more of a habit, but every once in a while I sink. Probably when I'm being all emo or something."

"Emo," Jordan repeated, his lips twitching with a hint of amusement. "Does that happen often? I mean, how much is every once in a while?"

Stefan crossed his eyes and stuck his tongue out at Jordan. "I'm young. I get to be pouty and bratty sometimes, and if I tell you how often, then where's the fun in that?"

Jordan laughed and Gideon did too—for a few seconds then he broke off suddenly. "How old are you, Stefan?"

Oh, that's a wicked, wicked look Stefan's got right now. Gideon's entire groin tightened with anticipation.

"How old do you want me to be?" Stefan purred.

Gideon's budding arousal went right out of the door at the same time that Jordan inhaled sharply. "What—" Gideon had to swallow back the question he'd been about to ask when Stefan smirked at him. "You're teasing."

"Duh, but you and Jordan both turned white as ghosts."

Gideon looked at Jordan. "What's that saying about being white as virgin snow?"

Jordan turned his nose up. "I haven't been a virgin in more years than I can count, and you're doing a fine imitation of ghastly yourself."

Gideon huffed but he couldn't keep up the act of being mad. Stefan still hadn't answered his question.

When he turned back to Stefan, Gideon knew he was waiting to be asked again. "I'm thirty-seven," Gideon started with. "Jo is thirty-four. How old are you?"

"Including the years I've been dead or not?" Stefan asked, amusement lighting his features. "Are we always the age we die at?"

"Don't go getting all philosophical on me," Gideon warned. "My eyes will glaze over and I'll doze off and drool."

Stefan giggled, covering his mouth with one hand as if to push the noise back inside.

"I like it," Gideon told him, nodding slightly. "That sound makes me happy."

"Makes me want to lay you out and kiss every inch of your body," Jordan supplied, which had Gideon frowning at his friend. That was a way better thing to say than 'that sound makes me happy'. Stefan was staring at Jordan with something close to awe in his pretty eyes.

"But we'd still like to know how old you are." Gideon hesitated, gnawing on the inside of one cheek. He let it go when it hurt like a mother to keep doing it. "Can you tell us how you died, or is that too…too much?"

Stefan's expression shuttered but he didn't leave them. "I'm twenty, or I was. Add over a decade to that now."

Gideon supposed years ceased to matter at some point once you'd died. He was glad Stefan had answered the question but he felt like he'd kicked a puppy with the way Stefan had closed himself off.

"I'm sorry for asking," Gideon said, which was true. He wanted to know, but now he wished he hadn't poked his nose into Stefan's business.

Stefan grunted and, after a long moment of silence, he seemed to shake off his funky mood. "Anyway, I didn't mean to go all weird on y'all. I don't like talking about what happened. Don't see the point in it."

But Gideon thought he saw fear flit across Stefan's features, and he wondered what could have happened to make Stefan so cautious. There was something about the way Stefan wouldn't meet his eyes just then that rang alarm bells in Gideon. He thought Stefan was scared, but of what? Pushing wasn't likely to get him any answers, not on the subject of Stefan's death. There were, however, other things he and Jordan needed to know.

"I want my clothes on," Gideon murmured, picturing not the uniform he'd worn earlier, but his favourite worn jeans, flannel shirt, and hiking boots. He threw in the idea of socks too and envisioned it all.

"Concentrate," Stefan said quietly.

Gideon did, even closing his eyes to visualise himself dressed as he wanted to be. He jerked at the sensation of his skin suddenly being covered, of his feet encased in comfortably broken-in leather shoes.

"Awesome!"

Gideon opened his eyes and grinned as he gave himself a quick once-over. "Yeah, thanks for the tutorial."

"Yes, thanks," Jordan murmured. Gideon peered at him and gave him a thumbs up.

"Love the white tank and tight jeans, Jo. Shows off your dick really nicely," Gideon informed him, eyeing that excellent package.

"That's why I picked 'em," Jordan informed him. "If you got it, flaunt it and all of that."

"Right."

Stefan scooted back on the bed, a sweet smile curving his lips. "Now, why don't you both join me?"

That was trickier. Gideon thought he'd never get himself settled on the mattress, but finally he was able to sit with an arm around Stefan's shoulders. Jordan was on the other side of Stefan and had one hand resting on Stefan's thigh.

* * * *

Stefan liked the way he fitted between the two men, but even more, he liked the budding camaraderie he sensed developing between him and them. There was already an established relationship of some sort between Jordan and Gideon, obviously, but he wasn't being excluded. He'd been afraid he'd blown any chance he had with these men after going all silent rather than answering about his death.

But Stefan had panicked. He didn't know how to tell them that he used to be different, that his brain had been damaged at birth and he'd been deemed developmentally slow and other similar things all of his living life. What if Gideon and Jordan were as horrified by that as they'd been in those seconds they'd thought he might be younger than he was?

What if they look at me like I'm damaged still?

Stefan wouldn't be able to stand it, so instead he sat between his new friends and explained as much about being a spirit as he could. He answered every question they asked in regards to that subject, and was glad they didn't bring up his demise again.

He listened as they shared war stories, appalled by the things mankind did to one another. Gideon and Jordan seemed to have made their peace with it all, but Stefan supposed that was what soldiers had to do in order to cope.

It was the tales about what they had done other than their duty that really perked Stefan up and gave him the opening he'd been waiting for. "Y'all really have shared guys before?"

Jordan and Gideon exchanged a glance before Jordan answered, his cheeks holding a faint blush. "Yeah. We each figured out the other one was gay when we got assigned to the same troop. Gideon wasn't as good at being unobtrusive when he was checking out other men as he'd thought he was."

Gideon snorted. "Right, like I didn't catch you beating off behind the showers one night after Craig walked out wearing one of those tiny towels."

Jordan groaned and rubbed at his package. "Come on, man. Craig was fucking hot, and the only reason you caught me was 'cause you were going back there to do the same thing."

"Yup," Gideon agreed.

"So y'all have been together for a while then?" Stefan asked.

Both men shook their heads. "Not like that," Gideon explained. "I mean, we fucked guys, together or singly, but we never messed around ourselves until earlier today. I don't bottom, and Jordan hasn't ever tried it, so he don't know if it's true or not, but he says he doesn't like it, either."

Stefan hoped he hadn't flinched when Gideon had brought up bottoming. Stefan wanted to get fucked again, but then he'd start getting scared when he really thought about it. Stupid, because he'd watched enough people to know that anal sex had to feel amazing when done with someone who cared about you. Still, Gideon and Jordan were hung like few men Stefan had seen even in porn videos. He was afraid having either of them fuck him would hurt no matter what.

"So you're saying you both like to fuck guys, but you don't let anyone fuck either of you." Stefan narrowed his eyes at Jordan then Gideon. "That hardly seems fair if there was ever going to be more than just a one-off with someone else." His heart pounded as he waited for reactions to his bold statement. Would he run these two off, or were they interested in more than a one-time fuck?

Gideon and Jordan looked at each other. Gideon finally shrugged. "I just don't like it. It doesn't feel good to me, but I suppose, if I were in a relationship with someone and it was important for them to get off like that, I'd do it and try not to be a jerk about it. I'd just hope the guys didn't want to do it often."

"Guys?" Stefan repeated, watching the way Jordan was staring at Gideon.

Gideon nodded. "Yeah, guys. I don't just play with Jordan and other men because it's fun. It's what turns my crank, having two bodies to touch, to lick." Gideon arched a brow at Jordan. "Maybe to fuck."

Jordan squirmed but he didn't look away. "I don't know. It's dumb, I know it is, but I always topped because I like the control."

"Bottoming doesn't make you weak." Even Stefan knew that. "Lots of really strong guys—physically strong and personality-wise—love a cock up their ass, as long as it's with someone they trust. Nothing wrong with it."

Jordan looked at Stefan. "So do you bottom, Stefan?"

Stefan's heartbeat tripled as he stared into Jordan's eyes. "Yeah," he answered breathlessly. "I think I want to."

Chapter Eight

Stefan's answer caused a strange sensation down in Jordan's lower anatomy. More specifically, his cock hardened and his own hole clenched. He was suddenly hyper-aware of his ass in a way he hadn't been before. Gideon traced a line down Jordan's nape and Jordan shivered.

"What about you?" Stefan asked as he rubbed his hands over Jordan's chest. "Are you rethinking the whole not bottoming bit? Your pupils are so dilated…"

Jordan closed his eyes but opened them again, gasping as his nipples were pinched.

"Stop hiding," Stefan commanded, the stern note in his voice surprising Jordan. "Just answer."

"Maybe," Jordan admitted. He was ashamed he'd thought bottoming somehow equalled being weaker. No, he'd used his own fear of letting anyone let that close to him permeate all of his sexual encounters. How many times had he secretly fantasised about having Gideon overpower him and force him to spread his ass open? Rape fantasies, and something

Gideon would never do, not if Jordan was fighting him, but it'd been the only way Jordan had been able to accept his own needs. He'd only ever dreamt of it with Gideon, but now, the image of Stefan, nude and hungry, that long, thick dick wet-tipped, was causing a riotous reaction in Jordan's body.

"I need to go check on Mom," Jordan blurted out. Knowing what he wanted and actually trying to get it were two different things. He needed a break. "You two stay here. I'll be back in a bit." Jordan shot out of there, trying the techniques Stefan had shared with them once he was out of the house. He practised diving and stopped, then he did the whole envisioning-where-he-wanted-to-go thing and ended up sitting on his mom's kitchen table.

Right in front of her, where she had her head bowed, cradling her face in her hands as she quietly sobbed.

Jordan forgot about his sex life issues. His eyes burned as he tried to comfort his mother. He reached for her, but hesitated when she raised her head and swiped at her eyes. Did she feel him there, somehow?

Jordan moved his hand slowly. When he had it hovering on his mom's shoulder, she closed her eyes and sobbed again. "Jordan."

He jerked his hand back, startled. Had that just been coincidence?

"I don't know if you're in heaven or if you're somewhere still on this Earth, if you're alone or if Gideon followed you like he tended to do in life." She cried for a minute and Jordan had to touch her again. He willed his hand to have some sort of substance, but every time his mom cried out, it broke his concentration.

"I never told you about the spirits here in McKinton," she said after several minutes, when she seemed to have got past a large wall of grief. "At first I didn't believe in them, and I didn't want you to hear the nonsense about them, either. I couldn't work them into my spiritual beliefs either, but I've seen things in the past years…" She shook her head and smiled. "Things that almost made me wet my pants. The spirits are real, and McKinton has plenty of them. I know it's selfish of me, but I kind of hope you're here."

Then she cried more, and Jordan focused, really focused, on the tip of his index finger. When his mother gasped and darted her glance all around the room, he knew he hadn't imagined the warm, soft flesh of her shoulder under his touch.

"Baby?" she asked, placing her hand where he was touching her. "Are you here? Are you okay? Are you happy?" She leapt up. "Severo!"

Jordan frowned, but it didn't take him long to remember the man his mother was now trying to call on the phone. Severo had come to McKinton right before Jordan had headed off to join the Marines. Jordan couldn't remember when exactly the other man had arrived in town — hell, Jordan had been a horny, self-centred kid. He hadn't paid attention to anyone other than himself at that time. But he did know who Severo was, and the resemblance of Conner's boyfriend to Severo was uncanny. He couldn't believe he'd missed it before.

Then again, he really only had a few memories of ever seeing Severo, and those times that he had seen the man, Severo had been in the company of the town sheriff, Laine Stenley. He didn't even know if Laine was still alive, if he was the sheriff or not.

"Thank you, Severo. I'll have coffee and there's plenty of food for you and Laine."

He supposed that answered his question in regards to Laine. Now that man Jordan had indeed noticed years ago. Laine was tall, stoic, a throwback to the days of Western cowboys who wore badges and kept their town clean with bullets and respect garnered by the residents. Yeah, Jordan remembered him very well. He wondered idly how the man had aged.

Jordan hovered in the kitchen while his mother got out dishes. She put small containers of sugar and some milk on a tray along with the cups and saucers. Then she went about making up a tray of lunch meats and cheeses, crackers and desserts. Jordan's mouth watered, but he wasn't the least bit hungry.

As his mother worked, she murmured to him almost constantly, filling him in on the town's events. Laine *was* still Sheriff, though there was talk that he wanted to retire and take his man off to Hawaii to live. And there were spirits—many of the people of McKinton had ended up having some kind of interaction with them. One spirit seemed to like to put on shows, send papers flying around and around like mini-tornadoes and other such harmless things.

Jordan was betting on that being Conner, though he couldn't imagine the guy being playful at that point. Not after Conner had gone all protective on Jordan and Gideon in regards to Stefan.

And thinking about Stefan caused all kinds of confusing feelings for Jordan. He really liked the kid— *No, not a kid.* Stefan probably would have been his age or maybe even older had Stefan not died. Jordan wasn't sure what the rules were with aging and death, or being dead, rather. He supposed he'd find out over time.

"Honey, it's just me," someone called out from the front room.

Jordan hauled his spiritly ass in there to see Craig Escobar closing the front door. Craig was the guy his mother was dating. Jordan had only got a few letters and emails from his mom about the man before being killed. He'd never met Craig since he'd only moved to McKinton in the past year.

Craig was short, and not just in comparison to Jordan's six-two. Jordan put him at five-five tops, which meant Craig was a couple of inches shorter than Jordan's mom. The guy was attractive enough, though. He had a round face that would keep him looking young forever probably, and distinguished-looking streaks of white in his hair at the temples. His clothes were nicely fitted designer jeans and top, but that was okay. He wasn't flashy, just well-maintained, Jordan thought.

And he looked at Jordan's mom like she was his entire world.

"Missy," Craig said almost reverently as he opened his arms to Jordan's mom.

She sniffled and moved into his embrace with an ease that bespoke of her own attachment to Craig.

Jordan wished he'd read those letters and emails more times than he had, that he'd looked for the love his mom obviously felt for Craig there in between the lines. He'd been such an idiot, missing what had to be there in her words. Jordan just hadn't been able to imagine his mom really with someone, but now he realised that, despite his age, when it came to his mom sometimes he still thought like a child. It was humbling.

"I've asked Severo to come over," his mother was saying, "and he's bringing Laine."

"That's nice of them," Craig murmured, rubbing Missy's back. "Is there a problem I can help with?"

She pulled back and swiped at her eyes. "Oh, no. There's not a problem, I just…" She took a deep breath, then exhaled slowly before moving away to lean on the counter. "Have you heard any stories about McKinton?"

Craig looked utterly confused. "Besides that it's one of the places to be in this oil boom?"

She nodded. "Yes, I mean about the town itself."

"I—" Craig closed his mouth and seemed to consider the question seriously before continuing. "I really am not around other people much. I mean, I work, running the business, and I go out to eat at the diner, thank God. Otherwise we might not have met. I'm pretty much a homebody, you know that."

"I do, but I thought maybe your employees might have talked," Missy said.

"About what?" Craig asked with obvious confusion.

"Ah." Missy crossed her arms over her chest and plucked at her sleeves. "Well, see—" She was saved from providing an explanation by a knock on the door. "Let me get that. Could you set the tray on the coffee table, please? Oh, and grab the coffee pot?"

"Sure, of course." Craig lifted the tray up while Jordan followed his mother into the living room. As she reached for the door, Jordan felt a frisson of unease spreading inside him. It wasn't that he sensed something evil, but more that he became aware of someone else sensing *him*. And he heard a male voice quietly ask in his head, *"Jordan?"*

Jordan flailed back as his mother opened the door. She greeted Laine and Severo, then stepped aside, giving Jordan his first look at the men.

Severo stared right at him with green-grey eyes that seemed to penetrate right into Jordan's soul.

Then Severo smiled, and there was such joy in the wide stretch of his lips that Jordan forgot to be freaked out when the man reached for him. He felt an electric tingle where Severo touched his shoulder.

"Missy." Severo didn't say anything else, just nodded, and Jordan's mom began to cry again. Jordan glared at the man. Severo was sexy for an older guy. He had long, straight black hair, and those eyes were something to write sonnets about. But Severo was watching him, and Jordan didn't understand how that worked.

"What's happening here?" Craig asked from behind him. "Why are you standing there with your hand in the air?"

Severo tapped his fingers against Jordan's shoulder then lowered his hands. "Craig, we met at the funeral."

"I remember," Craig said, walking right through Jordan. "What's going on?"

Severo looked at Laine, who shrugged and said, "It's your show, baby."

Craig didn't seem bothered by the two men so Jordan was leaning towards liking the man. He should have known his mom wouldn't date a bigot.

"Why don't we all sit down?" Severo asked as Craig looped an arm around Missy's waist. "Then we'll talk."

"Certainly." Craig turned and led Missy to the sofa. Severo looked right at Jordan again. More words seeped into Jordan's consciousness.

"I'm going to ask Conner to come here. I don't know if you've met him yet, but he's able to convince most doubters of the existence of spirits."

"How are you doing this?" Jordan finally thought to ask, or asked through thought, rather.

Severo hitched a shoulder and glanced up at Laine. *"I dunno. I just do it. I've always been able to speak to the dead."*

What was he supposed to say to that? Severo gestured and Jordan moved back, blending in with the wall as Laine brushed by him.

Jordan gawped at the man. He'd thought Laine was handsome years ago, but the years had carved him into a starker, more masculine visage than back then. He was almost fully white-headed now, and his sun-browned skin made him appear to be carved from mesquite wood. Jordan would bet the sheriff was every bit as tough and prickly as a mesquite tree, too. Some of those trees had branches with thorns on them that'd go right through the soles of your shoes. Jordan had got plenty of them stuck in his feet as a kid.

In the living room, everyone sat in awkward silence for a moment while Craig poured coffee and Missy passed around the snacks. Finally those niceties were out of the way and just in time, too, as Conner popped in. He wasn't alone, either. Jordan knew he had to be beaming with relief and something very close to joy when Gideon and Stefan popped in, too. He rushed over to join them, and wasn't surprised when Stefan hugged him fiercely.

"How sweet," Conner crooned just before he smacked Jordan on the back of the head, hard. "You hurt him, and I'll break you."

"Same thing he told me," Gideon muttered. Jordan looked up to see him rubbing the back of his head. "I didn't know we could get goose eggs."

Conner smirked.

Ro shook his head and pushed back a strand of his black hair. "Yeah, well, Conner's special like that. He can do things the rest of us mere dead folks can't. Yet."

"Ignore them," Stefan said as he released Jordan. "Conner is obviously compensating for something."

Conner's smirk vanished as he whipped his head around to glare at Stefan. "Boy —"

"Not a boy," Stefan said calmly. "And I don't need you to crack heads for me."

Stefan and Conner glared at one another.

"Wow, talk about tension."

Severo's words caused them all to look at the man. Severo held out an arm. All the dark hair on it was standing upright. "Like electricity in the air. Guess the egos don't die with the bodies."

Craig gasped. "How dare you —"

Laine turned a stony expression his way and Craig shut up.

"What are you talking about?" Missy asked.

Severo put his arm down. He turned to face Craig. "You don't feel it?"

"Feel what?" Craig retorted. "Awkwardness? Left out, like you all know a secret I don't?"

"That might describe it," Severo muttered. "What do you think happens when we die?"

Craig darted a glance at Missy. "Is this really an appropriate conversation to be having now?"

"Why not?" she returned with. "I'd like to know that Jordan was happy. Maybe he and his friend finally admitted they were in love with each other and they're —"

Jordan didn't hear the rest of her sentence because he was too busy panicking and trying to get out of the room. God damn it, he hadn't thought his mom would tell anyone his secret, ever.

Conner hooked his ankle with a strong grip. "Don't think so, you big chicken."

"Jordan?" Gideon's confusion was etched into the lines deepening on his brow. "She didn't mean—she just thought because we were friends, and both gay—"

Gideon's stunned expression said it all. Jordan had known he was more attached to his friend than Gideon was to him. He'd never have told Gideon, never.

Stefan placed a hand on his wrist. "It's okay. Friends love each other. That's part of being friends in the first place."

Stefan was giving him an out, and Jordan took it with both hands. "Right. She just took it to mean a different kind of love."

Gideon averted his face and Stefan moved to loop his arms around Jordan's neck. *It's going to be okay,* his eyes seemed to promise. Jordan rested his forehead against Stefan's. Stefan cuddled in closer and fitted perfectly to Jordan's body. Jordan closed his eyes and listened to the conversation amongst the living.

Chapter Nine

Stefan wasn't sure what was happening between him, Gideon and Jordan. After that encounter in his bedroom, when they'd all got on—and off—so well together, he'd thought maybe there'd be more messing around.

He'd thought wrong. Ever since Jordan's mom had spilled the beans, Stefan had been alone. Three days of it and he was ready to go sit in the graveyard and bawl like a baby. He hadn't realised how much he wanted something more with the other two men.

Maybe he should be grateful for what they'd done together and just let it go at that. Jordan, despite Stefan bailing him out when confronted about it, obviously had strong feelings for Gideon. Gideon had seemed absolutely shocked to hear it, but for all Stefan knew, they'd worked it out and were all in love and sappy with each other.

They probably hadn't even given Stefan a second thought. They'd had a heart-to-heart, exchanged promises of commitment and happily-ever-afters. Stefan would just be another guy they'd both shared for a short period of time. And Stefan knew he'd be alone again.

The thing was, he couldn't get Jordan and Gideon out of his mind. Even watching porn didn't work. Stefan wasn't interested in watching guys go at it online. He wanted the real thing, and he wanted it with two special men.

Stefan didn't hunt them down. He could have, easily, but he didn't. He hid out in his room for the first three days, moping and hoping. The hope part was for naught. Neither man popped in to see him.

By the fourth day, Stefan was done with brooding. He was over being broken-hearted, which, all things considered, he shouldn't have been in the first place. It wasn't as if he knew Gideon and Jordan. He'd barely spent any time with them. They were intriguing, handsome men, but they were done with him and he needed to get over it.

At least he knew now he could have meaningless sex. Sure, he felt a bit used because he hadn't expect to be so easily forgotten, but now he knew. He was nothing special, just a mouth-hand-hole-cock for guys. That was okay. He'd take it. Stefan wasn't going to keep being alone. If he could, he was going to find a different guy to waste a few hours with every night. Hopefully.

Stefan took off in the night sky, awed still by the beauty of the numerous stars twinkling so far above his head. When he'd been a child, he'd thought those were the souls of the people who'd died. His mom would tell him people went to heaven when they died, and she'd point up at the sky. Stefan had thought dying might not be so bad if he got to twinkle like that.

Dying had sucked, though. Fear, pain, humiliation—at least the way he'd died. It was hard not to think everyone was scared when their life was ending, but he'd heard there were people who accepted it calmly.

Well, the afterlife wasn't shaping up to be so hot, either. Sometimes he thought it'd be better, even, if he were still on the slow side so he couldn't think about all that he was missing.

Love, respect, sex. Sex. More sex. Well, he still felt twenty, and he was damned horny a lot.

Stefan rolled onto his back and tried to count the stars. It was hard to do when he was still moving.

Then he wasn't moving at all, because someone had a hold of his shoulders.

"Conner," Stefan began, thinking for sure his friend was messing with him.

"Wrong."

Stefan flailed and would probably have fallen had Jordan not kept a grip on him as he turned around.

"What are you doing here?" Stefan snapped, jerking out of the other man's hold.

Jordan flinched and tucked his hands in his pockets. He stared down at his feet, or the ground below them, Stefan didn't know. He certainly wasn't looking at Stefan.

"I wanted to see you," Jordan said gruffly.

Stefan snorted. "Right, after three, no, let's call it four days of nothing, you just thought you'd pop in when I *finally* decide to get over you and Gideon? Fuck you!"

Jordan whipped his head up so fast his neck popped. Stefan didn't care. The man's head could come right off and it wouldn't be Stefan's problem. He took off, leaving Jordan behind—only to yelp when he was tackled, Jordan's weight coming down on his back as strong arms wrapped around him.

"Don't leave," Jordan said quietly, and so seriously Stefan just knew he was getting the verbal accounting of all his fears. "Please."

"Fuck you," Stefan retorted again. "I don't owe you jack. You've had plenty of time to say anything you wanted to say, and you know what? You didn't. You didn't bother coming to me for the past few days, and I'm done waiting around!" All the time he'd spent thinking about Jordan and Gideon, wishing, hurting— damn it, Stefan was *mad*. And now Jordan was going to politely inform him that it'd been fun but all was done?

Jordan looked miserable, but Stefan dismissed it. He had to be reading the man wrong. Jordan's voice had a funny, strained sound to it when he spoke again. "You don't, but I owe you an apology, and an explanation. Please, I'll beg if you want, Stef, but please let me give you both."

Oh God. I'm pathetic. I should leave, tell him to fuck off, but I can't. I can't. The second Jordan had called him by a nickname, Stefan had known he'd cave in. He wanted Jordan and Gideon both to like him so badly. He wasn't going to let either of them hurt him again, though. Besides, hadn't he been thinking that the two of them had decided to be a couple instead of a threesome? Stefan wasn't eager to hear that confession, but he couldn't be a total ass.

"Fine. You can come with me to this club in Fort Worth. You'll probably find someone there to fuck. I know I will." Stefan grabbed Jordan's wrist. "I was going to take the long way and enjoy the night, but now I'm thinking speedy is the way to go. Close your eyes and picture me."

If Jordan couldn't manage it, then tough shit. He'd either pop up beside Stefan or not.

Stefan materialised in the seedy club. The music was loud and horrendous, but he didn't care. Jordan didn't appear and Stefan shoved his disappointment deep down inside. Jordan didn't want to be with him enough to be able to will himself to Stefan's side.

Fine. Whatever. Stefan was going to get on with his plan. There were plenty of spirits hanging around this particular club. Most of them were outright scary, but Stefan figured they couldn't do him much harm. Hurt him, sure, but he couldn't be killed again, could he?

No, just sent on to whatever was after the afterlife. Stefan stood up straighter as several pairs of eyes raked over him. He squared his shoulders and locked an emotionless expression in place. He dismissed the interest of men who didn't appeal to him. He was there for his own selfish pleasure, not someone else's.

One guy looked promising. Lean, young like Stefan, but there was a cruel twist to his lips as he sneered at Stefan.

Scorn was something Stefan could do without. He floated farther into the club and kept his nervousness hidden. At least, he hoped he did. Some of the men watching him made him feel distinctly like prey.

Going to a different club was becoming more and more appealing. Stefan had picked this one because he had hoped he'd get laid without much trouble. The thing was, all the male spirits there seemed like nothing *but* trouble.

When one of them grabbed him by the back of his shirt, Stefan spun around, swinging a hard fist at the guy's face. He wouldn't be anyone's victim ever again. His hand connected with a thud that rocked all the way back up his arm to his shoulder blade. It was jarring as hell for Stefan. How the other guy didn't go flying through the wall was beyond him.

Instead, his would-be groper only sailed back a few feet before growling and lunging forward. "You fucking little pansy punk-ass bitch!"

"Someone has a potty mouth," Stefan muttered. He caught the man's arm and ducked, flipping his psychotic admirer over his shoulder. "I never have liked dirty mouths, or their owners."

Stefan hardly had the chance to stand up before someone else came at him. He didn't even have time to think of being somewhere else before someone threw a punch at him. After a few more seconds of fighting, he didn't want to leave. This wasn't the kind of energy he'd come to expend, but it sure as hell was better than sitting alone hating the world.

* * * *

Gideon had looked all over the fucking world for Jordan—once he'd made up his mind not to let Jordan or himself hide from what they felt—and there the damned man was, floating in the night sky. *With Stefan.*

Gideon's cock hardened so fast his mind went blank for a second. He wanted Stefan, and, greedy him, he wanted Jordan, too. He hoped they'd both want him as well.

It looked like Jordan and Stefan weren't exactly happy with each other. Gideon could hear the anger in Stefan's tone. He saw Stefan grab Jordan's wrist, then Stefan was gone.

Gideon sped through the air and grabbed onto Jordan's ankles. He didn't want to risk the man vanishing on him again.

"Got you," he snarled, rolling and taking Jordan down with him. They fell through the air. Gideon wasn't afraid of them hitting the ground. They'd either sink or stop. He thought *Stop!* and they came to a rest inches above the grass.

"You're not going to keep hiding from me," Gideon all but shouted, anger burning hot up his spine and spilling out of his mouth. "I've fucking been trying to find you since you vanished out of your mother's house, Jo. You fucking left me! Just let her drop that bomb, let Stefan make an excuse for you, then you ran before I could even talk to you!"

"What did you want me to do?" Jo yelled right back, kicking and wiggling, never being still, making it hard for Gideon to retain his hold. But Gideon wasn't letting go. "I was so humiliated—"

"Because you love me, you ass? That's humiliating?" God, Gideon was going to explode with anger and hurt. "I'm that un-fucking-lovable?"

"Argh!" Jo shouted, throwing his head back and arching his thick neck. "You idiot! That's not what I said!"

"Both of you, shut the fuck up before I follow through with the bottle threat," Conner said, appearing above them. "Selfish, whiny fools. I told you what would happen if you hurt Stefan."

"Conner, calm down," Ro urged.

Gideon didn't let go of Jordan, but he did roll them both to their sides so he could see Conner and Ro too.

"Stefan is like my little brother, in case you haven't figured that out," Conner said, cracking his knuckles. "His living brother would love to tear you two apart, but, being flesh and blood, he can't do much. I, on the other hand…" Conner rolled up his shirtsleeves, baring muscular forearms.

"One at a time, promise me," Ro urged, watching them out of the corner of his eye.

"I'll take 'em how I can get 'em," Conner grumbled. "Come on, you chicken shits!"

Gideon didn't ask what they'd done. He didn't offer up an argument or a defence that they'd only known Stefan for hours. Conner was furious, and Gideon had to think the man was justified in being so, which meant that he and Jo had both hurt Stefan regardless of how long they'd known each other.

Which, considering how much he'd thought of Stefan while searching for Jo, Gideon understood. He was attached to the younger man, to his fine looks and bubbly personality. Gideon had intended to see if Jo would consider the three of them trying at a real relationship, but Conner wanted penance from them.

Gideon looked at Jordan, who gave the barest nod. "I'll go first," Gideon said before Jordan could offer. He let go of Jordan and shot up at Conner. Not to attack, but to make Conner think that was his intention.

Conner swung and Gideon's entire head reverberated with the pain of the impact. Conner's fist connected with his jaw, and Gideon saw stars, heard bells, thought his skull might have been knocked right out of his skin.

He went tumbling all over shoulders. Someone grabbed him by an ear—which was almost as bad as being hit again. Then he *was* hit again and Gideon's world went black.

* * * *

Jordan was really, really hoping Gideon wasn't dead-dead, as in gone on to whatever or wherever spirits went when they left Earth behind. He didn't know if they left some kind of ghostly husk behind or what, and that had been a hard blow Gideon had taken. There were things that needed to be said between them, and Stefan — Jordan couldn't just let him go.

Gideon hadn't even raised a fist to protect himself against Conner's wrath. Jordan wasn't sure he could let anyone beat him, even if he deserved it. Wallowing in his own self-pity for days might have cost him everything. Yes, he deserved to get his ass kicked.

Conner didn't wait for him to get up. Jordan was slammed into the ground with a punch that likely would have killed him had he been alive in the first place. *Jesus, Conner's pissed.*

He was grabbed again, pulled from the dirt and rocks and grass. Conner drew back to hit him again and froze, cocking his head.

"Shit!" Conner exclaimed. He tossed Jordan aside. "Stefan needs help!" And in an instant, Conner and Ro both disappeared.

"Stefan," Gideon rasped and Jordan shook his head. Gideon hefted him close. "Where's Stefan? He's in trouble."

Jordan didn't know, but he feared that he and Gideon both were going to be in for another round with Conner. "He said he was going somewhere to get fucked." Or to fuck. Jordan's bell was still ringing and he couldn't seem to get his mouth to shape the words without slurring them.

"How do we find him then?" Gideon said, his voice heavy with frustration. "Where is Stefan? He might need our help and I need to be there with Stefan — " And Gideon was gone.

Was that it? Jordan's heartbeat skipped as he replayed Stefan's earlier words and Gideon's. Did he just need to think about where Stefan and Gideon were? Or Stefan, because if Gideon did go somewhere else, would Jordan be split in two if he thought of following them both?

He shivered at the very idea of that. His head was pounding, his entire face ached, and he couldn't concentrate. Jordan closed his eyes and took several deep breaths. Judging by Conner's anger, he'd already failed Stefan once, at least. He'd hurt that innocent man—and despite any sexual experience Stefan might have had when he'd been alive, he was still innocent. It showed in his touch, in his expressive eyes.

Jordan bowed his head. Stefan had been so hurt, so angry. It had surprised him, because they hadn't known Stefan long, and Jordan had convinced himself the connection he'd felt with Stefan had been one-sided. He'd been wrong, hadn't he?

Where was Stefan? Jordan concentrated around the throbbing in his temples. The sounds of the night seemed to grow louder, crickets, cicadas and the occasional passing vehicle trying to disrupt his attempt at focusing.

Knowing Stefan might be in danger stiffened Jordan's resolve. He pictured Stefan, the way he felt, the sounds he made, let the longing to hold the man flow through him.

There was a *whoosh* of air and darkness so complete it seeped through Jordan's closed lids. Then there was a cacophony of sound, and someone hit Jordan on the other side of his jaw.

Jordan roared with pain and opened his eyes as he went on the attack. He caught sight of the shitty bar they were in, of the dozen or more spirits embroiled in a massive fight. Conner's bellow was followed by one man rocketing past Jordan. Another followed shortly thereafter.

Jordan started swinging.

Chapter Ten

He might have made a mistake. Stefan could admit that much. And fighting wasn't as much fun once you took a few punches. Still, he was kind of stuck. He couldn't concentrate long enough to get away because people kept trying to hurt him.

Yeah, he'd really screwed up. He couldn't be killed, but he was going to be hurt so badly that he'd probably wish he'd die. There was definitely evil intent in more than one man's eyes.

Stefan screamed and kicked, he hit and bit, anything to keep them from pinning him down. Desperate, he yelled for Conner, hoping to be saved, and God, how he hated that he needed to be saved.

What was wrong with him? All he'd wanted was to get laid, to get past his past and to forget about the two men who'd hurt him almost as badly as Johnny had hurt him. The intense, instant connection he'd felt for Gideon and Jordan was obviously unrequited. Stefan wasn't going to keep agonising over it.

Conner came through the place like a whirling dervish, hitting and slinging Stefan's attackers. Ro was right behind him, but as soon as one spirit went flying, two more seemed to appear.

Stefan thought it was like some minions from hell, except he didn't believe in hell so he had to assume there were just a lot of evil assholes hanging around the club. And he'd led his friends right to them. "Shit."

Punching and clawing got him closer to Conner. Ro was back to back with his man. Stefan was grabbed from behind and flung backwards, a kick catching him in the ribs. He howled with pain and saw red, so furious at himself, at the bastards who wouldn't leave him and his friends alone, at Gideon and Jordan for not wanting him.

Stefan went wild, tearing through the place, a whirlwind of betrayal and rejection. Years of repressed emotions spilled out of him, splattering his anger on his opponents via his fists.

It built up and spewed over, a volcanic eruption of hate he'd carried since he'd been able to think, since he'd come to understand he was *different*. It didn't matter if his physical brain had gone on to wherever and his spirit was normal, he'd always felt tainted by his living form.

No wonder Jordan and Gideon hadn't wanted him. Someone probably had told them about Stefan's lack of mental acuity when he'd lived. They might have just figured out he was weird on their own, too.

It all hurt, and Stefan was so tired of hurting, tired of covering it all up—his insecurities and doubts, his memories and regrets, all of it. He'd had enough of being the bright, happy sidekick. God damn it, he wanted to hurt the people who had hurt him.

Or so he thought, until he saw Gideon and Jordan, bruised, bleeding—he didn't even wonder on that—

each man barely standing under the onslaught of attackers. Guilt slammed into him at the same time that a fist connected with his stomach. Stefan's breath gusted from his lungs as he doubled over.

He saw the boot coming for his head, someone kicking at him. He threw out one hand, trying to block the blow. The kick never landed as the man was grabbed and thrown in the opposite direction.

Gideon, panting, furious, grabbed Stefan under the armpits and yanked him upright.

"Home," Gideon snapped.

Yes, Stefan wanted that too, and he wanted Jordan with them. Every part of him ached, some parts throbbed and others seemed like they were screaming from pain. Stefan wanted comfort, he wanted to pretend at least for a while that he mattered to someone as more than a friend or brother.

He wasn't sure what had happened. His mind was racing with images of Johnny mocking him, fucking him, killing him, and the crazy sons of bitches from the bar. So many mean people in his head. Stefan didn't want to remember any of them.

"Shh, sweetheart. It's okay."

Oh God, now I'm delusional too. No one spoke to him like that, like he really was special.

"Stefan, open your eyes for me," someone else said. Stefan knew those voices, Gideon's rougher one first, then Jordan's. He had to be dreaming.

Soft touches to his shoulders and face made him whimper. He wanted to be cared for so much that the lack of it hurt worse than the physical pain he felt from the fight.

"Come here," Gideon rumbled. Stefan didn't know what he meant and figured Gideon must be talking to Jordan since Gideon still had an arm around Stefan.

But Gideon might not have been talking to Jordan, because the warm, hard length of Gideon's body was suddenly pressed to Stefan's entire backside. He shivered as Gideon's breath wafted over the sensitive skin of his neck.

"I have you," Gideon whispered just as another body pushed against Stefan's front. "Me and Jo, we have you. We're not letting you go until we figure this out."

Stefan didn't have the energy to argue or express his disbelief. There was no point in doing so anyway. He knew this was all a dream. He'd wake up by himself, just like he had all his life.

* * * *

Jordan knew the instant Conner appeared. The air in the room seemed to grow frigid. Gideon grunted and Jordan raised his head up to find Conner, looking like he'd never even been in a huge brawl, glowering above them.

"Let him go," Conner snapped, the temperature dropping even more.

"Conner," Ro began, tugging on his arm. "Calm down. All you're going to do is make Lee and Darren's whole house unbearably cold. Why would you want to do that?"

Conner growled and flung his hands up. "I don't want to! I want to toast these two bozos' asses and toss them out of McKinton!"

Gideon turned his head a few inches. "No."

"No?" Conner mimicked.

"No," Jordan added. "You don't get to do that. If Stefan wants us to go, then we will." Jordan didn't want to leave his mother behind, but he wouldn't hurt Stefan again.

"He won't want either of you here after the way you've hurt him," Conner informed them. "Selfish fuckers."

Gideon sat up a bit, but kept one hand planted on Stefan's hip. "It's not your place to judge us. What happened between the three of us, that's our business, but I can assure you we didn't break any promises to Stefan."

"No, you just broke his heart," Conner snapped. "Or his hopes, at least. Maybe he wasn't all googly in love with y'all, but he's been alone for so long, and I've watched him for years, wanting someone of his own. Waiting for someone to see how amazing Stefan is, to appreciate him and to be trusted by him. Stefan's past—"

"Is my business," Stefan cut in softly. "It's my business only."

Conner's entire expression shifted from furious to loving. "Right, Stef, it is, and you don't owe these two fools anything, okay?"

Before he could do anything to stop it, Jordan was pushed aside and held against one wall. Gideon hit the opposite one with a thump. Conner stood with his arms extended in their directions, power oozing from him. He only had eyes for Stefan.

"I know you hate being alone, Stef, but don't settle for anything less than you deserve, and contrary to what you might think, you deserve to be treated like a goddamned treasure." Conner moved over and sat beside Stefan.

Jordan still couldn't unpin himself from the wall.

"You can't blame yourself for how you were born," Conner began.

"Stop," Stefan pleaded, sitting up and grabbing onto Conner's shoulders. "Please, just stop."

Conner cocked his head and stared back at Stefan. "You're ashamed."

Stefan looked away.

Jordan wondered what the hell Stefan had to be ashamed of. Jordan looked at Gideon, who glanced at him in confusion then focused on Stefan.

"No, you have no reason, Stef." Conner pulled Stefan into a hug. "You don't. All this time, you've hated yourself for it and I didn't even see it."

"I don't hate myself," Stefan whispered, clinging to Conner. "I just hate *that* about myself."

"Oh, baby," Conner sighed. He buried his nose in Stefan's hair and began rocking him from side to side.

Jordan itched to shove Conner out of the way and to hold Stefan himself. He suspected Gideon was experiencing the same want. Somehow, they were going to work everything out. Stefan needed them, and they needed him.

* * * *

Seeing Stefan in Conner's arms was maddening. Gideon wriggled and tried to free himself. He was stuck against the wall like a damned moth pinned in place. Conner was a freak—a scary, strong, protective freak.

Conner glared at him over Stefan's head. Gideon snarled and began to struggle harder. Maybe if he kept fighting, Conner would tire of holding him still. He couldn't seem to get any words out, either. Conner's smug look was the most annoying damned thing Gideon had ever seen in his life.

Gideon glanced at Jordan. *Fight,* he thought. *Don't be complacent. We have to fight for Stefan, or...* Gideon examined Conner's expression closely. There was more than just smugness there. Granted, Gideon could be wrong in his reading of the other man, but he thought there was hope and expectation in Conner's bright eyes.

And he got it. Conner *wanted* them to fight him. Not necessarily physically—because they'd already got their asses whooped by him, and even though neither Gideon nor Jordan had fought back then, Gideon knew there was no hope in trying to do so. Conner would simply put them down every time they got up until they had to quit.

So then he *didn't* want them to fight *him.* Understanding dawned like someone turning on a light switch. Conner wanted them to fight for Stefan, even if that meant fighting *with* Stefan if he pushed them away.

Gideon got it. He'd have said so but Conner was still doing his creepy control thing. Adrenaline rushed through Gideon's veins. He needed to be free, at least to speak if nothing else. Stefan out of Conner's arms would be good, too.

Conner out of their lives while they sorted everything out would be fan-fucking-tabulous.

Gideon drew on that need to be with Stefan, on the desire to touch him and to touch Jordan as well. They needed to talk, they needed—each other, the three of them. Whatever Stefan was hiding in his past, it was past. It was time for it to stop causing him to suffer.

Gideon pictured it in his head, him holding Stefan, Conner turning into a wisp of annoying vapour that smelt roughly like sulphur. The added stink was fitting in his mind as Conner was annoying the devil out of him. Ro would need to disappear too, but he could just go. Gideon wanted Stefan between him and Jordan. They should be the ones comforting him.

"Fuck—" Conner's shocked voice had Gideon peeking out from barely opened lids. As he watched, Conner faded away, his mouth moving but no sounds coming out.

Gideon hoped he didn't send him anywhere bad. Kind of.

"Conner!" Stefan shouted, but Gideon caught him before he could shoot up to try to go after Conner. Gideon wrapped himself around Stefan and caught Stefan by the chin. He saw a flash of fury in Stefan's eyes, heard the beginnings of a curse word being hurled at him.

Gideon slanted his mouth over Stefan's. He swallowed every foul word the man loosed at him, and held him as Stefan battered his shoulders and back.

But Stefan didn't pull away. He didn't bite or kick.

He didn't turn Gideon out, or demand that he leave. Gideon hoped the tantrum was cathartic for Stefan. He delved his tongue deeper into Stefan's mouth and ran one hand down to grip a softly rounded ass cheek.

Immediately after he felt the press of Jordan's cock against the back of his hand. Jordan reached around and held onto him with one hand. The other was pushed between Gideon and Stefan.

Stefan whimpered and the hitting turned to clutching instantly. Gideon tilted his head and ramped up the heat of the kiss, demanding everything Stefan would give him.

Stefan opened for him like a man who was starving for loving. From what Gideon had heard, that was accurate. He kneaded the flesh under his hands, touching his men. They would be his. Gideon wasn't letting either of them go.

Jordan could fucking well deal with his embarrassment over his mom spilling the beans. Gideon loved the silly fool right back, and Stefan— Stefan had the power to wrap him and Jordan both around his pinky.

Gideon wedged a knee between Stefan's legs. He pressed his thigh up, pushing Stefan's balls up. "Ride it," he rasped, turning his head aside. "Come on, let me feel you on me."

Stefan whimpered and began rutting. His clothes disappeared and Gideon thought that was the best idea yet. He willed his clothes gone and one look told him Jordan had done the same thing.

Gideon leaned around Stefan enough to get to Jordan's mouth. He was afraid—Jordan could reject him, refuse to be kissed, but Jordan opened beautifully for him.

The three of them rubbed and touched each other. Gideon traced Stefan's crack, pulling his ass open.

Stefan whined and tossed his head. Gideon and Jordan had to end their kiss, but Stefan's pleasure was worth it. Stefan humped Gideon's leg frantically. Jordan grabbed Stefan's cock and gave him something to fuck.

Gideon found the tight little aperture nestled between Stefan's butt cheeks and he rubbed over it.

"Oh God!" Stefan shrieked right before he shuddered. His cum was hot and fragrant as it spilled from his cock. Gideon kept touching his hole until Stefan stopped shaking. Then he kissed Stefan, tasting his pleasure, needing to find his own.

Jordan had to be hurting, too, so Gideon would wait. He plundered Stefan's mouth, owning him and giving himself in return. Stefan keened then went still. Gideon hadn't closed his eyes all the way, wanting to watch Stefan's expression as he came apart, and now something like trepidation was scampering over Stefan's features.

"I'm not going to fuck you," Jordan said from behind him. "Just…this. Gonna do this, if you'll let me."

Stefan's expression shifted to one of borderline bliss. Gideon peeked over his shoulder and nearly came on the spot as he watched Jordan dragging his cock up and down Stefan's crease. The slick moisture making his dick glisten had to have been Stefan's own spunk.

"Fuck," Gideon ground out.

"I remember what he said," Jordan panted out. "He was going to fuck, not get fucked."

Gideon took a minute to process that. All he could reason out was Jordan meant Stefan had told him he was going to that fucked-up bar to fuck someone, not get fucked. Jordan wouldn't fuck him unless Stefan wanted it.

Gideon wanted to fuck them both, and he wanted to watch Stefan take Jordan, see him open up Jordan's ass slowly, stretching him and making him beg to be filled.

Jordan bit his bottom lip then released it. He paused in humping Stefan's crease long enough to say, "You're thinking dirty, dirty thoughts, Gid. What are they?"

Stefan hissed and wiggled his butt. "Don't stop," he said over his shoulder before looking back at Gideon. "What? Tell us."

Gideon reached for and found Stefan's cock, already growing hard again. He fisted the base. "I want to see this in his ass."

Stefan wasn't the only one who moaned at that. Jordan's hungry sound convinced Gideon he'd get to have his wish, sooner rather than later.

"Ever had anyone suck your cock?" he asked Stefan.

The squeak he got in answer was adorable.

Gideon slid down Stefan's body. He didn't draw out the torment. Stefan had never had a blow job, and that was all kinds of a shame, but it was also thrilling to Gideon, knowing he'd be Stefan's first. He sucked the crown past his lips and swirled his tongue under the ridge.

Stefan mewled and clawed at his head. Gideon reached beneath him. He let go of the base of Stefan's shaft so he could fondle Stefan's balls. With his other hand, he palmed Jordan's balls from between Stefan's legs.

Jordan cursed and began fucking Stefan's crack faster, driving him against Gideon. That was fine with him, he wanted Stefan to go to town on his mouth. He sucked strongly and Stefan yelped. He thrust his hips and Gideon hummed his approval, wanting more.

Stefan gave it to him, bucking without rhythm, instinct driving him after the ecstasy Gideon's mouth was promising him. Gideon almost gagged as Stefan's cock breached his throat, but almost as soon as it was there it was gone again, Stefan withdrawing and shoving back in part of the way.

Gideon gave both of his men's balls a squeeze. Jordan's shout rang out right before Stefan's. Spunk jetted into Gideon's mouth. He swallowed eagerly once he let the flavour of it permeate his senses.

Then he was being pushed back, and he didn't know or care where he was going to land because Stefan was on him, licking and sucking at the tip of his shaft.

Jordan straddled Gideon's chest and tapped his lips with his softening, wet cock. "Open."

Gideon did, gasping as Stefan suckled him hard. Jordan thrust inside, the girth of his dick bringing an ache to Gideon's jaw.

Gideon looked up at Jordan, pleading silently for him not to leave again. Jordan grunted but he gave the tiniest of nods before fucking Gideon's mouth.

Stefan cupped Gideon's balls. He took a good half of Gideon's length into his mouth then he came back up. He fisted the lower half of Gideon's cock before proceeding to suck him in again.

Gideon hollered around the mouthful of cock he was sucking on. Jordan framed his face, holding onto Gideon and staring into his eyes as he drove repeatedly into his mouth.

When they'd been living beings, they'd both had incredible stamina, but now Gideon thought he could fuck all day and night and not have to stop. Stefan and Jordan must have felt the same. Stefan had come twice already, but Gideon was pretty sure he was feeling Stefan rubbing a third erection against Gideon's calf.

And Jordan was close to coming again, his cock swelling, that thick vein throbbing beneath Gideon's tongue. Jordan tightened his grip and snarled as he drove himself into Gideon again and again. At the same time, Gideon's dick was encased in such silky hot suction that his brain was surely scrambling.

Then a press of a fingertip to his hole sent him over the edge. No one ever touched him there, hadn't for years and years. To feel a timid, bare touch was more stimulating than Gideon had ever remembered it being.

He tried to shout, but his mouth was stuffed full. Jordan did, though, bellowing and pumping his load over Gideon's tongue. All Gideon could do was shake and moan as his climax tore him apart with a thousand strands of pleasure.

He was vaguely aware of Jordan pulling his cock free. Gideon's vision was blurry and he was achy in spots from the physical fighting of earlier, but he honestly didn't think he'd ever been happier in his entire life than he was right then.

Chapter Eleven

He was going to have to tell them. Stefan pried open his eyes. They were cuddled so perfectly together, the three of them, but Stefan's conscience was kicking him in the gut. He sat up and both Gideon and Jordan grumbled.

The two men were battered, bruised — though not as badly as if they'd been alive. Still, they'd got those marks trying to protect him. He touched the worst one on Jordan's cheek.

Jordan opened one eye. "Fuckin' Conner," he groaned.

Stefan cocked his head. "Conner?"

Jordan moaned and rolled onto his back. "Yup. Guy can throw a punch."

"'Specially when we aren't trying to duck 'em," Gideon said from Stefan's other side.

Stefan frowned back and forth at them. "What are you talking about? When did Conner do this, because I saw Jordan right before I went—" Well, maybe bringing up the whole bar thing wasn't a good idea.

"Before you went looking to get some ass," Gideon finished bluntly. "If we hadn't been such self-centred dicks none of that would have happened. I'm sorry, Stefan. I didn't think you'd believe I'd just blown you off."

"Same here." Jordan sat up and ran a finger over Stefan's bottom lip. "I mean, you're the guy I want to take my cherry, baby. That ought to tell you something."

It ought to, but Stefan was kind of in a state of disbelief.

"I think you shocked him into silence." Gideon sat up and began kissing the back of Stefan's neck. "Not even a squeak out of him. I'm glad you've decided to give butt sex a chance from the other end of things before saying it isn't for you."

"I—" Stefan squeezed his eyes shut. The vision of him pushing his cock into Jordan's hole made him whimper. He had to open his eyes up and grab the base of his cock. A hard grip kept him from coming. "I haven't ever done that."

"Oh, two virgins," Gideon murmured. "That means I'll get to direct."

"He does love to watch," Jordan added.

"Love to do, too," Gideon said.

"I've been fucked before," Stefan reminded them, fearing they'd forgotten and would think him a complete virgin. Both men turned expectant looks on him, with Gideon moving around to be able to see his face. "It hurt. Both times."

"Twice only?" Gideon rasped. "How long ago?"

"A long time ago," Stefan whispered. "Right before he killed me." Stefan hung his head, ashamed of his past. His life.

"Wait," Jordan snapped. "You're saying the guy who you had sex with…killed you?"

Stefan nodded without raising his head all the way up. "Yeah. I was stupid. I just wanted someone to want me. It was just a game to him, then he didn't want anyone to find out he'd ever played it."

"What the fuck?" Gideon said, not quite yelling but with enough anger that it gave Stefan goosebumps. "He killed you to keep it a secret? Did he rape you?"

Stefan looked up then, just for a second. "No, no, I wanted him to…to want me. I just didn't understand what that meant."

Gideon narrowed his eyes and Stefan averted his gaze again.

"And how long have you been a spirit?" Jordan asked.

"I'm not sure exactly. Twelve years, ish, like I said before."

"Were you raised in some kind of a religious compound where you didn't know about sex or—"

"I was mentally retarded," Stefan interrupted, not wanting to make them keep coming up with more and more ridiculous postulations.

The silence in the room was telling. Stefan slid out from between the two men. "My brain, something happened when I was being born. It was a physical thing, though, see? And when I died, the physical died too. All that was left was my spirit, what made me, me. But I get that I'm still—"

He stopped. He was still what? Stefan scowled. He wasn't still limited by the physical. What he was limited by was his own memories and shame. Conner was right, of course. Stefan hadn't had any choice in how he'd been born, but he couldn't stop feeling like a complete fool for letting Johnny touch him.

"I was so pathetically desperate," he whispered. That was what he couldn't forgive himself for.

"Everyone wants to be loved." Jordan came over and Gideon did, too. "We want to be loved, and we want to love and feel good. I don't care how you were in your lifetime, Stefan. I like the man you are now."

"Did you think that would make us not want you?" Gideon asked.

Stefan shrugged.

Gideon caressed Stefan's cheek. "I think you're an amazing man. I want to kill the guy who hurt you."

Stefan flicked a hand. "Oh he's dead. Someone killed him in prison, after he was convicted of killing me." Stefan finally held his head up then, but he looked up at the ceiling, unable to meet his lovers' eyes. "I was afraid he'd end up being a spirit, and finding me, but Conner... Conner said he took care of that. I don't know how, and I don't want to. Conner's just Conner. He wouldn't let me get hurt again."

"Except we hurt you," Jordan muttered. "I was embarrassed and scared because... "

Stefan had to look at him, just *had* to.

Jordan smiled shyly. "I didn't think Gid wanted me to love him. We acted like friends, never touched each other until after, you know, we were killed. I—" He glanced at Gideon and gulped before going on. "Gideon's the only man, other than you, that I'd let fuck me. I've thought about it, a lot."

Gideon burned with a wantonness that was unmistakable. He didn't move, though, just watched Jordan hungrily.

"I thought he'd think less of me," Jordan continued. "Especially if I told him I wanted him to fuck me. I was stupid. Figured since Gideon didn't let anyone top him, he'd think I was weak for wanting it, and even weaker for falling in love with him." He held up a hand when Gideon opened his mouth. "I didn't know you'd tried it several times and hated it."

Gideon snapped his mouth shut and nodded.

Stefan frowned at him. Gideon didn't like getting fucked? "Did it hurt a lot?"

Gideon paled. "No, I just didn't like it. It didn't feel good, and when the guys I tried it with rubbed against my prostate, I wanted to kick them off me. It just—I wished I liked it. I do." He arched his eyebrows. "Do you think maybe, since it was a physical thing, I might like it now?"

Stefan felt flushed from his forehead to his toes. "Maybe?" he eked out. He thumbed in Jordan's direction. "He can try. I'm scared I'll screw it up and you already said you hated before so I don't—" Oh God, he was babbling. Stefan bit his tongue too hard and yelped. "Oh thit," he lisped, pressing his tongue against the roof of his mouth to stymie the pain.

"Bite your tongue?" Gideon asked, looking too smug for Stefan's liking. Stefan turned his nose up at the man. "For what it's worth, I think you're sexy when you start getting nervous and ramble on."

Stefan swallowed loudly as he fought back the urge to jump Gideon and fuck him, or be fucked. He didn't care, either was seeming like a really good idea.

"I'm sorry your first sexual partner was a murdering bastard," Jordan said, "But if you'll let us be your last two, I promise you won't regret it, right, Gid?"

"Right," Gideon agreed quickly.

Stefan checked his tongue. The sting was gone. He was still afraid to take the next step despite his rampant hormones.

"What's wrong?" Gideon asked.

"Your past doesn't matter, except that it matters to you," Jordan added. "It made you into the man you are."

"But—" Stefan had to force the words out, because he was afraid he'd make a point that would result in Gideon and Jordan leaving him and going on together. He had to say it, regardless. "You love each other, and I'm just here."

Jordan hissed and Gideon spared him a wink. "Why would you doubt it, Jo? I followed you here. I've always followed you, except when you followed me."

"You never said," Jordan groused.

"Because you didn't say, and I was too scared to do it first," Gideon explained. "Then we died, and guess what? Life really is short, but I'm hoping the afterlife is long, so we all three have decades and decades to spend learning and loving each other." Gideon surprised Stefan by hooking an arm around him and pulling him close. He stared down into Stefan's eyes in a commanding way that made Stefan feel quivery inside. "As for you, we haven't known each other long, but I can promise you this. I've never been so drawn to anyone before, and I know Jo hasn't either. There was never a man we both wanted as much as, it turns out, we want each other. Until you, Stefan."

Gideon kissed him softly, so tenderly that Stefan's eyes burned as emotions welled up inside him. Hope that he might really be wanted, that there might be love some day between the three of them—Stefan couldn't refute it and didn't want to. He wanted his happy ending, and he wanted it with these two men.

"I won't lie and say I'm in love with you," Jordan said as he took Stefan from Gideon's arms. "Easy words with little weight to them are blown away in the first little storm that comes along." He tipped

Stefan's chin up with two fingers. "But like Gid said, I feel more for you than I ever have anyone else after such a short period of time. Even Gid. Honestly, he intimidated me." Jordan winked at Stefan. "And he's kinda gruff at times, but you…"

Jordan licked his lips, then he licked Stefan's and moaned softly. "Oh God, you're just… Stefan, you're more than I ever hoped for, and that you're willing to have us both? So amazing, baby." He licked Stefan's mouth open and plunged his tongue inside.

Whereas Gideon's kiss was a show of tenderness, Jordan gave Stefan need and craving. His desire for Stefan was clear and bright as he pulled Stefan closer.

"Most beautiful sight ever," Gideon said. "I need to touch you both." He wrapped his arms around them both while Jordan continued kissing Stefan senseless. "Mm, look at you two. Never thought I'd have this."

Stefan's head was spinning when Jordan let up on the kiss. Jordan touched Stefan's lips. "Look at them, Gid. Swollen, red, perfect for sucking cock, don't you think?"

Stefan flicked a glance at Gideon, who was studying him closely.

Gideon shook his head slowly. "Parted while he's panting and fucking you would be better right now."

"Fuck," Jordan scraped out. "That. That one."

Gideon grinned. Stefan felt his lips curving up in a matching smile.

Gideon rubbed his hands together then began stroking his own dick. "We're going to have so much fun."

"Right after we have a word."

Gideon pivoted around and Stefan groaned, rolling his eyes.

Conner stood, looking very fierce and…scowly, Stefan decided.

"Conner, can't it wait?" Stefan pleaded.

Conner studied him for a moment. "Did you tell them?"

"Yes, Dad," Stefan whined. "Go away. I don't want you watching."

Conner's smile was wicked enough to scare the devil himself. "Oh, baby boy, fair's fair. How many times have you watched?"

"You watched Conner and Ro?" Gideon and Jordan both asked, sounding shocked.

Stefan's cheeks were so hot with a blush that he thought he might just turn into a human—or spirit—torch. "Yeah, and he knew it. Some of the others, probably not." He shrugged. "I was bored, and I'm not the only one who—"

Gideon kissed him until Stefan's eyes crossed.

"Guess we'll just have to keep our man too busy to spy on anyone else," Jordan said.

Stefan broke the kiss long enough to speak. "I don't watch anyone anymore. I haven't—" Gideon plundered his mouth until all Stefan could do was whimper and cling to the man.

"So what did you want, Conner?" Jordan asked. "Because we're about to be very busy for a few days. Or longer."

Oh God! Days! Stefan hoped Jordan wasn't exaggerating.

"Just wanted to make sure y'all had all made up, really," Stefan heard Conner say. "I'm going to leave y'all to it."

"Adios," Jordan told him. "And we won't forget. We won't hurt Stefan, ever again."

"Good. Nice dick," Conner said, and Stefan opened his eyes just in time to see Conner vanish.

"Did he mean mine, yours, or yours?" Jordan asked, pointing to Gideon then Stefan.

Stefan looked down at his shaft. "He's seen mine before. Clothes are no big deal sometimes."

"I think he left it at that just to see if he could stir up an argument between the three of us," Gideon grumbled.

Conner's laughter filtered into the room, then it was gone.

"Asshole." Jordan shook his head, then he laughed. Stefan and Gideon joined in, and Stefan felt free from his past in a way he hadn't been able to before.

Chapter Twelve

"Do we have lube?" Gideon asked as he led them outside. "Do we need lube?"

Jordan looked at Stefan, who seemed unsure.

"I have an idea," Gideon purred. "Let's find a nice, moonlit field, and I'll handle the rest."

"I know a place," Stefan offered. "Come on."

Stefan was right, clothing wasn't always a necessity. There was something particularly naughty about being outside and nude, even if people couldn't see them. They took off, running in the air, laughing and groping, Jordan happier than he could remember being in ages.

Stefan squealed when Jordan goosed him, getting a good handful of that sweet ass. Jordan wanted in there, but first, he wanted to give Stefan his promise of forever. Silly, sappy, romantic—Jordan figured he was all of those things. He was more than okay with it.

Stefan veered around a grouchy-looking old man on the sidewalk. He went through a couple of other people, laughing when one of them paused and looked around furtively. "Some of them feel us, I think," Stefan offered, then he shot up into the air.

Jordan and Gideon were right on his tight little tail. Literally, with both of them touching his ass every chance they got. Stefan giggled and tried to dodge away, but Jordan rolled under him and latched onto Stefan's dick. With his mouth.

"Ack!" Stefan shrieked, stopping on the spot. "Don't stop!"

Jordan didn't, as it made no difference where they were having sex, really. In the air, on the bed, it was all the same. They could float or not, and right now, he wanted to make sure Stefan floated right on into orgasm.

Gideon got behind Stefan. "Lean over," he urged.

"What—" Stefan panted and curled over Jordan's head. Jordan had a damn good idea of what Gideon was doing, and in seconds he was proven right as Stefan yelped and began undulating.

Jordan knew Gideon was spreading Stefan's cheeks and licking that sweet ass.

"I haven't," Stefan began, "I—can't… Would—"

Jordan thought the babbling was adorable. He sucked Stefan's cock in to the base and Stefan moaned, the sound deep and raw.

He reached around to tangle his hand with Gideon's on Stefan's ass. Gideon tugged his hand over, positioning it so that Jordan could feel the wet skin of Stefan's hole.

Stefan wasn't the only one who liked that. Jordan groaned around the long, thin cock in his mouth as he pushed his fingertip against the tight ring. Gideon's tongue licked over it, then Gideon pressed the tip of that slick muscle into Stefan's pucker.

At the same time Jordan took Stefan's shaft into his throat. He swallowed around it and slid his finger in alongside Gideon's tongue.

Even the living souls had to hear Stefan's scream as he came, jerking and shaking so hard Jordan halfway expected him to fly apart. He eased his finger out and away from Stefan's opening as Gideon shoved his tongue in deeper, eating Stefan's ass like it was the finest dessert and Gideon's sweet tooth was insatiable.

Stefan came so much Jordan thought the poor guy was going to be emptied out for a day or two, but Stefan's dick never did go soft in Jordan's mouth.

Jordan didn't ease off until Gideon pulled Stefan back. Stefan was shivering and breathing unsteadily, his eyes closed and those red lips of his even more swollen, as if he'd been biting at them.

Stefan's eyes flew open as he gasped. He arched his back and Jordan scurried around to Stefan's backside to see what was being done to him. Gideon grinned wickedly and hooked an arm around Stefan's waist as he thrust a finger in and out of Stefan's hole slowly.

"Like this, sweetheart?" Gideon asked, gaze locked on Jordan.

Jordan nodded, his own ass feeling empty, needy.

"Yes," Stefan said in a voice deepened by need. "God, never felt anything so good."

"Oh?" Gideon slid two fingers in.

"Ah," Stefan moaned, spreading his legs. Then he jolted and hissed.

"Not even that?" Gideon asked. "Because that's your prostate gland right...there."

"Jesus holy hell!" Stefan shouted, bending over to grab his knees. "Again!"

Gideon chuckled and repeated the touch until Stefan was slamming back onto his fingers. "Yeah, this is gonna feel so good around my dick," Gideon said, his shaft looking painfully hard. "I'll fuck you so good you'll weep."

Jordan would have scoffed at the line except for the fact that Stefan looked close to tears now, so desperate for release as he writhed and moaned.

But Gideon withdrew his fingers. "Soon. Get us there. I want to watch you take Jordan."

"I want to feel him take me." Jordan was well past eager to be fucked. Not just by Stefan either, but by Gideon, too, whenever Gideon was ready for him.

As for Gideon wondering about having his ass played with and taken, well. Jordan already had a plan.

* * * *

Stefan couldn't get them to the field he had in mind fast enough. He couldn't concentrate to pop over to it, either, because sex was about all that was on his brain.

But he got them there, to a field where grass waved and rolled in the evening breeze. Trees were scarce, but that was fine. They didn't need them. The moon was only a hangnail moon, as his momma used to call it. Stars blinked all over the night sky.

"Beautiful," Gideon murmured, but when Stefan turned around it wasn't the sky that Gideon was looking at.

Stefan ducked his head down and looked through his lashes at Gideon. "Thanks."

Gideon reached for Stefan with one hand and Jordan with the other. He tugged them together and Jordan took over, bringing Stefan close and kissing him.

Gideon began licking down Stefan's spine. "Gonna show you how to do this so you aren't scared about fucking Jo."

Stefan was nervous about that, but he trusted Gideon and Jordan. Gideon had already showed Stefan how good it could feel to have something in him down there.

But Gideon wasn't done. He nibbled and sucked his way down Stefan's crack while Jordan kept kissing him. Jordan found Stefan's nipples and rolled them between his thumbs and fingers.

Stefan moaned into Jordan's mouth and hung onto Jordan's biceps. He needed to feel more, from both of his lovers.

"Get him wet, Jo," Gideon stopped lapping at his backside long enough to say.

Jordan nipped Stefan's lip then sank down to suck his dick again.

At the same time, Gideon inserted two moistened fingers into Stefan's pucker. He was still stretched and damp, and the thickness was a welcomed weight inside him.

Gideon fingered him slowly while Jordan blew him. Stefan tried to cant his hips and get Gideon to rub his prostate, but Gideon bit his right buttock in warning. "Be still," he added.

"Yessir," Stefan replied cheekily. That got him a smack following the bite and he wiggled his backside again.

"You don't want to come before you get to fuck Jo, do you?" Gideon asked. "I know you'll get hard again, but wouldn't you rather fill Jo up with your spunk, make that virgin ass of his all yours?"

Stefan stilled and so did Jordan, rolling his eyes up to plead with Stefan.

And Stefan understood that he was in charge of this part of their connection. He cupped Jordan's jaw and tugged, urging him to come up. Stefan kissed Jordan fiercely — then nudged him up higher. He wrapped his arms around Jordan's powerful thighs and buried his nose in the thick golden patch of pubes around Jordan's cock.

"Please, baby," Jordan begged. Stefan stuck two fingers in his mouth and got them good and wet. At that moment, Gideon, evil man, lightly touched Stefan's gland.

Stefan growled down at him and Gideon chuckled. Then he pushed another finger in, stretching Stefan's hole wider.

Stefan coated his fingers as much as he could while his synapses were shorting out from pleasure. Gideon pulled his digits free and licked instead at Stefan's cock. It was really wide, the head especially. Stefan clenched around Gideon's fingers while bringing his own around to zero in on Jordan's pucker.

Jordan moaned and hitched one leg up, opening himself to Stefan. It was a show of trust and need that moved Stefan like little else could have. He rubbed over and over Jordan's tight muscle, trying to get it to relax enough to slide a finger in. He took Jordan's cock into his mouth, sucking hard.

Jordan gasped and his sphincter clenched. Stefan poked and his finger went into that constricting heat.

So soft, Stefan thought, then Gideon touched his gland again and began pushing those digits into him faster, harder. Stefan had to fight to keep his eyes open, to concentrate on not shooting his load yet.

Then Gideon pushed a fourth finger in, slowly, but the burn was almost too much. Just when Stefan feared he'd have to ask Gideon to stop, pleasure began chasing away the pain.

Jordan cursed and gyrated his hips. Stefan got the message. He began pumping his finger in and out while sucking on as much of Jordan's cock as he could take. Gideon kept his movements to a bare minimum, and Stefan knew he was just waiting for Stefan's ring to stretch a little more.

Then... Stefan shivered, wanting that 'then' so badly. He sucked Jordan harder and worked a second finger into him.

"Stefan, please, fuck me," Jordan got out in between huffed breaths. Before Stefan could answer, Gideon withdrew his fingers.

"Now," was all that Gideon said.

Stefan released Jordan's shaft and left off fingering his ass. He would have turned Jordan around, but Jordan shook his head. "Weightless, right?"

"Yeah, but—"

Jordan climbed up on Stefan, bracing his hands on Stefan's shoulders. "Hold your cock up for me." Jordan locked his legs around Stefan—No, Stefan realised. Gideon was helping to support Jordan's legs.

Then Stefan's thought's sputtered as he heard Gideon spitting, heard him rubbing skin on skin. Stefan didn't look back as his pulse raised. He thought he knew what was happening. Gideon was using spit to slick up his cock.

"Yes," Stefan hissed, finally having to close his eyes as he used a hand to hold his cock up.

"Yes," Jordan repeated as he pushed himself down, taking the first few inches of Stefan's cock before stopping. "Oh hell, that feels so weird."

That threw Stefan off. He opened one eye. "Weird bad or weird—Oh my God!"

Gideon nudged Stefan's hole with the wide hard tip of his cock. "Gonna let me in?"

"Good weird," Jordan answered, closing his eyes. "Fuck, yeah, definitely good weird."

Stefan's thoughts scattered as his pucker gave under a sharp thrust. There was a slight burn but Gideon had stretched him well.

"Oh my God, oh my God, oh my God," Stefan babbled, his head lolling on his neck as pleasure flitted from every nerve ending in his ass to all the others throughout his body.

"Yeah, yeah," Jordan agreed, bouncing up a bit then shoving himself all the way down on Stefan's dick. "Fuck!"

"We are," Gideon muttered, then he reached around and took a hold of Jordan's ass. "All of us." He sank his cock into Stefan's hole, steadily filling him up.

Stefan keened and thought he was dying all over again, but this was an ecstatic death, everything in him alight with more pleasure than he thought he could bear. His cock was encased in such perfect, gripping heat that he couldn't even comprehend it, and his own hole was stuffed so full he couldn't even clench around Gideon's shaft.

Then Gideon began moving, fucking him with shallow, forceful thrusts. Each one drove Stefan's hips forward, shoving his dick into the wonderful grip of Jordan's velvety sheath. They repeated this dance between the three of them until Gideon began putting more power into each movement.

Stefan held onto Jordan as he fucked the man harder, faster. Jordan shoved a hand down between them and fisted his own shaft.

Gideon snarled and sucked a spot on Stefan's neck that made him cry out. Gideon chuckled, then he bit that same spot.

Stefan didn't stand a chance against the triple onslaught. He bucked and screamed, his cock pulsing out his release into Jordan's eager hole.

Jordan slammed their mouths together, a painful hot kiss that was brief because Jordan was writhing, cursing as he shot his load onto Stefan's belly and chest.

Gideon pounded into Stefan's ass, nothing gentle about the way he was taking Stefan. He folded Stefan over, Jordan sliding off him and dropping down to lap at Stefan's balls while Gideon ploughed into him repeatedly.

His cock kept dragging over Stefan's gland in and out, in and out. Stefan was melting, coming apart under the rapturous feelings Gideon was fucking into him.

Then Gideon grunted and shoved in even deeper, grinding against Stefan's ass. Stefan's shaft gave a little squirt of cum as Gideon jerked Stefan back even harder on Gideon's dick.

Gideon's jizz marked Stefan inside. He felt every jet of it painting his inner walls while Jordan kept licking at his sack. Gideon held Stefan in place with hard hands on his hips. He writhed against Stefan for what seemed to be several long moments, but Stefan couldn't be sure. He was toast, wrung out and thoroughly fucked.

Gideon finally stilled. He draped himself over Stefan's back. "God damn, your ass is a treasure for sure. Just like the rest of you."

"Gotta work on your cheesy lines," Stefan managed to say before he forgot how to speak. He wasn't sure he'd ever move again.

"Y'all love my cheesy lines," Gideon informed him. "Jordan, you still licking his nuts?"

"Mmmhm," Jordan said around a mouthful.

Stefan's libido decided it wasn't down for the count after all. Gideon chuckled and moved his hips. Stefan's eyes shot open. The man's shaft wasn't softened at all.

It was going to be a long, fun night.

Epilogue

"I can't believe Mom is getting married." Jordan shook his head. "I can't even walk her down the aisle."

"Sure you can," Stefan said, looking at him like he was an ace short of a deck. "Just tell Sev you want to. Since Craig quit trying to talk her out of believing in the existence of spirits, you can't really have anything against him."

Gideon snorted. "Yeah, but it took Conner wrapping Craig up in a sheet, suspending him in air, and carrying him outside for everyone in town to see in the middle of broad daylight, with a nice balmy temperature of forty degrees surrounding Craig."

"It worked." Stefan didn't think anything else mattered in regards to Conner's methods. "And you know the saying, the hardest people to convert are always the strongest believers once they give in."

"Isn't that about religion?" Jordan asked.

"Stefan's right, seems applicable in any situation," Gideon agreed. He looked out of the window. "Supposed to be a full moon tonight. I heard a little birdy mention that our field had nice, tall grass again."

"About fucking time," Jordan snarked. "If that Mr Rademaker mows our field down again, I'll haunt him until he moves."

"We don't even get in the grass, much," Stefan pointed out. "Well, okay. Sometimes we do, but it grows back fast."

"I don't care." Jordan crossed his arms over his chest. "I don't like him messing with it."

"Maybe we can get Sev to mention it. We'll ask him when we talk to him about your mom's wedding." Stefan moved over to sit on Jordan's lap. "How was your mom today?"

"Good. Still talking away at me. She told Sev she just knows when I'm there, and I have to think she does."

"Did you do the hair thing on her?" Stefan asked.

Jordan shook his head. "I'm afraid it might freak her out."

"Why would it?" Gideon sat down beside Jordan. "She knows. Maybe it'd give her comfort instead. She seems good, though. Saw her smile the other day."

"Yeah." Jordan's smile was a carbon copy of his mother's. "She's doing a lot better. I can't imagine being in her shoes, losing a child, but you know. She's always been an amazingly strong woman. She knows I'm happy, and she approves of you two."

"Of course she does," Stefan said. He fluttered his lashes at Jordan. "I mean, come on, we're pretty freakin' marvellous!"

Jordan laughed. He had to agree. His lovers were pretty freakin' marvellous indeed.

"Love you, baby," he told Stefan, taking a quick, hot kiss.

"Love you too," Stefan replied, before exchanging the words with Gideon.

Jordan would never get tired of this, and he'd never take his men for granted.

* * * *

"Oh look at her, she looks so beautiful," Stefan said, dabbing at his eyes as Missy appeared at the entrance of the church.

"She does," Gideon agreed. Jordan waved to them, beaming as he began escorting his mother down the aisle.

It didn't matter that she couldn't see him. She knew he was there. Sev had worked with Jordan, and so had Conner, to make sure he had a substantial enough mass that Missy could feel him even if it was only as light touches at her side.

Her eyes shone with joy and Craig watched her like she was the most precious person in existence.

Stefan had two men who looked at him that way, and he was pretty sure he looked at them just as sappily.

He had never expected much out of his life, and maybe he'd expected even less out of his death.

But someone somewhere had been watching out for him. Stefan didn't know the whys and hows of it, but he'd been chosen to be the recipient of Gideon's and Jordan's love.

It was worth dying for, and even more, Gideon and Jordan were worth *living* for, in the afterlife and anything that might come next.

About the Author

A native Texan, Bailey spends her days spinning stories around in her head, which has contributed to more than one incident of tripping over her own feet. Evenings are reserved for pounding away at the keyboard, as are early morning hours. Sleep? Doesn't happen much. Writing is too much fun, and there are too many characters bouncing about, tapping on Bailey's brain demanding to be let out.

Caffeine and chocolate are permanent fixtures in Bailey's office and are never far from hand at any given time. Removing either of those necessities from Bailey's presence can result in what is know as A Very, Very Scary Bailey and is not advised under any circumstances.

Bailey Bradford loves to hear from readers. You can find her contact information, website details and author profile page at http://www.totallybound.com.

Totally Bound Publishing

www.ingramcontent.com/pod-product-compliance
Lightning Source LLC
Chambersburg PA
CBHW030137180626
46812CB00002B/735